*It was a kiss th[at held the same]
whispered promise as the snow.*

The promise that something wonderful was on its way—if only the right flakes could fall at the right time.

"That probably wasn't the wisest thing to do." Jessica's voice shook a little on the last syllable, the only betrayal that she had been as moved by the moment as he.

"No, it wasn't," C.J. agreed, reminding himself that his priority right now was his daughter. Kisses—and what they might hold down the road—would have to wait.

"But it did prove one thing."

"What's that?"

"That a little something unexpected can sometimes be very, very nice."

Dear Reader,

I am a total Christmas-aholic. I start right after Thanksgiving. I have my tree up almost as soon as my turkey is put away. I'm out there shopping at the early-bird sales, blasting Christmas music in my car. I love everything about the holiday, from the snow to the gift wrap.

I had the joy of writing this book during December, which gave me an extra boost of Christmas spirit. So, as you're reading Jessica and C.J.'s story, know that I was stringing my own lights and wrapping gifts in between writing scenes.

Another thing I love at Christmas is chocolate. But I have little time to cook (too much shopping to do, of course), so I thought I'd share my easy Crock-Pot chocolate recipe:

Shirley's Easy Chocolate Peanut Clusters

2 pounds white almond bark (also called white baking bar)
4 1-ounce squares bittersweet chocolate
12 ounces semi-sweet chocolate chips
24-ounce jar honey-roasted peanuts

Put all ingredients in Crock-Pot; cook 1 hour on high. Stir occasionally to prevent burning on the edges. Turn Crock-Pot to low and stir every 15 minutes until thoroughly melted and combined. Using a tablespoon, drop onto waxed paper in clumps sized to fit in your mouth. Leave to cool. Remove from paper and either freeze for up to 3 months or put in covered containers and store unrefrigerated for up to a week. Makes 4 dozen (or less, if your drops are bigger).

These are really good. Mine rarely make it to the New Year, because my family loves them.

May your holiday be filled with wonderful memories, and may your year ahead include lots of great books to read!

Shirley

SHIRLEY JUMP
Miracle on Christmas Eve

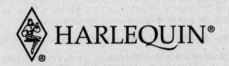

TORONTO • NEW YORK • LONDON
AMSTERDAM • PARIS • SYDNEY • HAMBURG
STOCKHOLM • ATHENS • TOKYO • MILAN • MADRID
PRAGUE • WARSAW • BUDAPEST • AUCKLAND

ISBN-13: 978-0-373-03990-6
ISBN-10: 0-373-03990-5

MIRACLE ON CHRISTMAS EVE

First North American Publication 2007.

This edition published by arrangement with Harlequin Books S.A.

www.eHarlequin.com

Printed in U.S.A.

New York Times bestselling author **Shirley Jump** had neither the willpower to diet, nor the talent to master under-eye concealer, so she bowed out of a career in television and opted instead for a career where she could be paid to eat at her desk—writing. At first, seeking revenge on her children for their grocery-store tantrums, she sold embarrassing essays about them to anthologies. However, it wasn't enough to feed her growing addiction to writing. So she turned to the world of romance novels, where messes are (usually) cleaned up before The End. In the worlds Shirley gets to create and control, the children listen to their parents, the husbands always remember holidays and the housework is magically done by elves. Though she's thrilled to see her books in stores around the world, Shirley mostly writes because it gives her an excuse to avoid cleaning the toilets, and helps feed her shoe habit. To learn more, visit her Web site at www.shirleyjump.com.

Praise for Shirley Jump...

"*Rescued by Mr. Right* is appealingly different, relying on the strength of its narrative and characters rather than a hook."
—*Romantic Times BOOKreviews*

"Jump's office romance gives the collection a kick, with fiery writing."
—*PublishersWeekly.com,* on *New York Times* bestselling anthology *Sugar and Spice*

"Shirley Jump gives a thoughtful and insightful story with *The Other Wife.*"
—*WritersUnlimited.com*

To my children, whose wide-eyed wonder makes every Christmas absolutely magical. And, yes, I do have a lot of fun making you two wait to open your presents—but even more fun watching the joy on your faces. I love you guys. You're the only Christmas present I ever need.

And to Bill and Janice Roe, a real-life Mr. and Mrs. Claus, who provided the inspiration for this story.

CHAPTER ONE

JESSICA PATTERSON was done with Christmas.

No buying of a pine tree that would shed all over her wall-to-wall carpet. No hanging of a festive red-bowed wreath on her front door. And no candy cane cookies on a gaily decorated platter with dancing snowmen who sported goofy stone-created smiles under their little carrot noses.

She'd done enough Christmases. No more, not for her.

"Where's your red suit?" Mindy Newcomb, her best friend for ten years, leaned against the counter of Jessica's toy shop, arms crossed over her chest. "It's December nineteenth and you haven't even taken it out of the attic yet. The town Winterfest is in three days. And you don't have so much as a paper snowflake in the window. What's wrong with you?"

Jessica straightened a display of white teddy bears set up in the center of Santa's Workshop Toys. The pale color was all the rage this year in stuffed pals, so Jessica had made sure to stock up. "I told you, I'm not staying here for Christmas this year. I have a round-trip ticket to Miami Beach, a mega bottle of SPF 45 and a brand-new Speedo. I am *not* putting on the Mrs. Claus suit because I will not be here."

"I really thought you'd get over this by now."

"What do you mean, over this?"

"This…mood you've been in." Mindy waved a vague hand. "Come on, Jessica, you love Christmas."

"I *used* to love Christmas. I don't anymore." The clock chimed ten. Jessica crossed to the door, flipped the sign to Open then headed to the register and checked for the right ratio of quarters and nickels. She knew to start the day with a lot of small change, particularly now that school had let out for Winter Break. The children of Riverbend would be in soon, spending their allowances on the myriad of small items laid out on the dime and quarter table, biding their time until the ho-ho-holiday with super bouncy balls and new sets of jacks.

Mindy slid onto the stool behind the counter. When Jessica joined her, she laid a hand on her friend's, her eyes welling with sympathy. "I know the holidays have been pretty hard on you since Dennis died."

Jessica nodded and swallowed the lump in her throat. Two years and yet there were days when it felt like yesterday. "Christmas just isn't the same without him." She glanced at the pictures on the wall, a collection of images featuring happier days with Mr. and Mrs. Claus—Jessica and Dennis Patterson.

They'd started soon after they'd married fifteen years ago, donning the suits with padding, then as the pounds crept up on Dennis, he hadn't needed the extra pillows. He'd looked good as he rounded, like a teddy bear she could curl into.

But those very pounds had been his undoing, putting a strain on his heart that it couldn't handle. Yet he'd kept the doctor's warnings from her, ignoring the ticking time bomb in his chest because he loved being Santa. Loved his life. And hated anything that would put a crimp in it. He'd been all about being jolly—and never about anything serious.

She'd loved that about Dennis, until she realized that was the very thing that had cost her the man she loved.

Every year, they'd played the Mr. and Mrs. Santa roles, delighting in the smiles on the children's faces as they'd handed out toys and candy canes, putting on a real show at the annual Riverbend Town Winterfest. They'd posed for pictures, even built a sleigh and set up a little decorated house—a glorified shed, really—in the town park, where children could come and spend a few minutes visiting with

Old St. Nick, telling him what they wished to see most under their Christmas tree.

After Dennis had died too soon at forty-eight, leaving Jessica a young widow at thirty-seven, she'd carried on the show for one more year, for the memory of her husband, for the kids they'd loved. But those kids had grown up. And the ones she'd seen in the past couple years hadn't exactly been the Norman Rockwell version of Christmas spirit.

Jessica turned away from the pictures. "The whole thing stopped being fun a long time ago. Besides, I lost my Christmas spirit after Andrew Weston defaced my Frosty."

"He was just a kid, pulling a prank."

"Mindy, he painted him green and hung him from the oak tree in the center of the town lawn. Said he was releasing Frosty into the wild or something. Then that Sarah Hamilton…" Jessica shook her head. "I try never to think badly of a child, but that girl knows exactly how to get on my nerves."

"She is a bit of a—"

"Brat," Jessica finished, then immediately felt bad because Sarah was really only a product of her unconventional upbringing. "And that's not a word I use lightly."

"She's been through a rough time, Jess. She only lost her mom, what, two months ago?"

Jessica sighed and sank onto the second stool. "I

know. I don't think she has any family left. She's been living with her babysitter, which has to be hard on her." Sarah had taken to hanging around the store after school a lot lately, asking questions, always wanting Jessica's attention at the busiest possible times. Driving Jessica nuts—and pitching a fit if she didn't get Jessica's undivided attention when she wanted it.

"If she had a dad, he's not around." Mindy's lips pursed in annoyance with the missing father who would leave his child stranded like that. "And Kiki never even said who he was."

"She *was* an odd duck, wasn't she?" Jessica thought of Sarah's mother, who'd waitressed at the downtown diner and had died her hair a different color to suit her different moods. Rough and outspoken, Kiki had stuck out in Riverbend like a hammerhead shark in a tank full of angel fish.

Having Kiki for a mother explained a lot about Sarah's behavior. Jessica knew enough about the woman to know the words *schedule* and *discipline* weren't in her vocabulary. For a woman like Jessica, who'd lived by a schedule for more than three decades, Kiki's life wasn't just unusual—it was crazy.

"Sarah's had a difficult life," Mindy said, "between living with Kiki and now being practically orphaned."

"And normally I'd be all sympathy and cookies."

Guilt once again knocked on Jessica, and she vowed not to say another bad word about anyone, and especially a child. "But this year, it's like I've run out of patience. Every time a kid comes in here, I'm tense and annoyed."

"That's not like you."

"I know. Plus, the kids aren't the same, Mindy. They don't believe like they used to. Kids today are…" Jessica threw up her hands.

"Jaded. Angry. Pierced and tattooed."

Jessica laughed, but the laughter wasn't filled with humor, it was dry and bittersweet, touched by longing for the old days. For Dennis's patient touch, his understanding of kids, his year-round love of the holiday season. *He* was the one who had embodied Christmas, not her. She'd gone on last year, for his sake, his memory, but she hadn't had his ability to create the same magical spell. To pull something out of nothing. "Yeah. Dennis and I always said that when this stopped being fun, that was when it was time to hang up the red suit and white wig."

She slipped her hand into the space beside the register and withdrew the pamphlet she'd picked up at Olive's Outlandish Travel that morning. Even Olive had given her a look of disappointment as she'd handed over the round-trip ticket and the brochure, but Jessica remained resolute.

"*This* is where I need to be for Christmas," Jessica said, further cementing her resolve to leave town. "Pristine white sand. Gentle, lapping waves. Hot sun baking on my skin. Cabana boys bringing me drinks with little umbrellas." She pointed at the picture of a Caribbean paradise, then ran a finger along the words printed at the bottom of the resort's advertisement. "And especially this. 'No small children allowed.'"

"But you love kids. You love Christmas."

Jessica shook her head, refusing to be dissuaded from her plan. Next thing she knew, she'd be handing out candy canes and posing for pictures. The adults in Riverbend might miss the extra entertainment at the Winterfest, but Jessica wasn't fooling herself into thinking the children would notice one way or the other. The town seemed to have lost its sparkle—or maybe she had. Either way, playing Mrs. Claus wasn't on her agenda, not this year. Maybe not ever again, especially without a Santa by her side to add that extra spark of magic. "My mind is made up and my bag is packed. I'm leaving tomorrow."

Mindy rolled her eyes. "There's nothing I can do to talk you into staying? To being Mrs. Claus one more time?"

Jessica laid a hand on Mindy's and looked her best friend straight in the eye. "Honey, I wouldn't be

Mrs. Claus again if the big guy himself came all the way down from the North Pole and got down on his knees to ask me."

Christopher "C.J." Hamilton had only one purpose for his visit to Riverbend, Indiana—to give his daughter, Sarah, the best damned Christmas ever.

Whether she wanted it or not.

To that end, he'd brought along a whole bunch of presents, and a determination to create a holiday she'd never forget.

Even if he had no idea what he was doing. Holidays weren't his forte. He had about as much experience with Christmas as most people did with camel jockeying. But he had a little girl who needed a miracle and that was motivation enough.

The problem? He barely knew Sarah. She didn't know him at all. The last time she'd seen him, Sarah had been three days old. And C.J. had thought walking away was the best decision.

Actually, the only possible decision. Kiki had sat in her hospital bed and told C.J. with a straight face that he wasn't the father, breaking his heart even as he held Sarah's precious, talc-scented body in his arms, then watched another man walk into Kiki's hospital room and be pronounced Daddy.

He'd been stunned when the lawyer had tracked him down on location in Costa Rica last week, telling him Kiki had died in a car accident…and lied about her child's DNA roots. He was the father, and he was expected to come get his daughter, create insta-family and take one more problem out of the lawyer's hands.

C.J. had started by calling Sarah, thinking he'd ease into the dad thing. She'd refused to come to the phone. He'd tried to call her twice more on the trip from California to Indiana, and both times, she'd been as mute as a roll of gift wrap.

Then, he'd stopped by to see her at LuAnn's apartment, and Sarah had run and hidden, refusing again to talk. "Maybe pick her up a little present," LuAnn, the babysitter, who lived in the apartment next door to Kiki's and who had taken Sarah in while the lawyers looked for a blood relative, had suggested. "Ease into it. She's really a darling girl."

A darling girl who'd already made it clear she wasn't interested in having C.J. as a dad.

C.J. stopped the truck outside the small toy shop in downtown Riverbend. In the window of Santa's Workshop Toys was a tiny, hand-lettered sign that read Home of Mrs. Claus.

Perfect.

This place, he'd been told, was where the heart of Christmas lay—and not to mention had become a favorite hangout of Sarah's. "You talk to Jessica Patterson," LuAnn, a lifelong resident of Riverbend, had told him, "and you'll get your Christmas. She *is* Christmas in Riverbend."

C.J. was counting on it. His experience with the holiday was about nil. He needed an expert.

C.J. got out of the Ford F-250, then went inside the shop. The bell overhead let out a soft peal announcing his arrival.

Once his eyes adjusted to the interior, he stopped and gaped. The toy shop had to be every child's dream. Stocked floor to ceiling with bright, colorful dolls, trucks, blocks, games and every imaginable plaything, it sported a rainbow of decor, hanging mobiles of planes and animals, and had a Santa's workshop theme running throughout, with little elves perched on the shelves and an entire North Pole village painted on the far wall. It looked…magical.

His Hollywood trained eye admired the care in the details, the imagination in the design. No wonder Sarah loved the place. If C.J. had been twenty years younger, he'd have spent all day here, too.

"I'm just about to close up," said a voice in the back.

C.J. paused among a bunch of Slinkies and rubber dice. He toyed with a gyroscope, spinning the little wheel. "I'm not here to buy anything," he called back. "I'm looking for Jessica Patterson."

"You've found her."

He looked up. Hoo-boy. If this was Mrs. Claus,

then he definitely needed to revisit a few of those Christmas tales. Jessica Patterson was tall, with long blond hair and green eyes that seemed to dance with light. She had a lush, red mouth and a curvy figure that redefined the word *hourglass.*

She was, in other words, very hot for someone who was supposedly hailing from the most northern region of the world.

"*You're* Mrs. Claus?"

"Only at Christmas," she said, laughing, and putting out her hand to shake his. "And not anymore."

He took her palm with his own, feeling her warm skin against his own and decided that there was nothing cold at all about this woman. "What do you mean, not anymore?"

"I am officially hanging up my Mrs. Claus suit this year. But if you need a stuffed bear or a jack-in-the-box or—"

"No. I need you." C.J. looked around the shop and realized a toy—hell, a whole truckload of toys—wasn't going to do it. To win Sarah over, he needed something big. *Really* big. And according to LuAnn, there was nothing bigger than Mrs. Claus, at least in Riverbend.

She dropped his hand and moved back. Wariness filled her features, dimmed the friendly light in her eyes. He might as well have stamped his forehead with Serial Killer. "You need me?"

"In a purely professional sense. As Mrs. Claus."

"Sorry, but I can't—"

"You have to. I've got a reindeer on order and everything." Okay, now he really was sounding crazy. C.J. drew in a breath. "Let me start over. My name is Christopher Hamilton. Also known as C.J. the Set Construction Wizard." He turned and pointed out the window at the bright-red script written across the door of his pickup truck, saying the same thing along with a California address.

"And what does a set construction wizard want with a Mrs. Claus? Because I don't do movies, if that's what you're thinking."

"No, I'm not here for work. I'm here for my daughter. I need to give her an incredible Christmas."

"So take her to a mall, put her on Santa's lap. Listen to her tell him what she wants, then put whatever that item is under the tree." Jessica turned away and busied herself with straightening a shelf of board games.

C.J. didn't have time for her to get the Scrabbles sorted out from the Monopolys. "I've heard you are *the* person to see for Christmas. And, lady, believe me, I need a Christmas." Right now, because he had a short time frame, an impossible daughter to win over and a major life change to deal with. He didn't want to wait on a board game.

"You can find that anywhere, Mr.... What did you say your name was?"

"Hamilton."

She paused, a checkers game halfway to its proper place on the shelf. "You're *Sarah's* father? But I thought…"

She didn't finish the sentence and he didn't blame her. Most people he'd run into since arriving in town—from the gas station attendant who'd given him directions to the building super who had let him into Kiki's apartment—had looked at him, added two and two and automatically labeled him as a bad paternal figure. "I'm here for Sarah now, and that's what counts. Isn't it?"

"Yes, yes. Of course."

"The only thing she wants—and what she deserves this year more than anything—is a good Christmas." He didn't mention that he had zero parenting experience, had yet to get his daughter to talk to him, that LuAnn had told him the girl's melancholy increased every day, or that he was counting on Christmas to help him build a bridge to a six-year-old stranger. A miracle on so many fronts, even he had lost count. "She never really had one. Will you help me give her one or not?"

The woman before him hesitated, smoothing a hand over the game's black-and-red cover, avoiding his gaze. But most of all, the question.

Jessica Patterson was right. He could take Sarah to a mall. To another town. He could, indeed, find his

Christmas anywhere. But he wanted to create those happy memories here, in the town where his daughter had had so many unhappy ones. He wanted to turn the tide for her, to show her that there was, indeed, a rainbow behind all those clouds.

And if he could pull off that miracle, then maybe, just maybe, there was hope that he could be the dad he needed to be for the years ahead.

Because he hadn't been much of one up until now. And he had a lot of ground to cover between here and December twenty-fifth.

For that, C.J. suspected, he was going to need a lot more than a reluctant blonde in a red suit.

CHAPTER TWO

JESSICA TUCKED the striped one-piece bathing suit into her bag, did a final visual check, then shut the suitcase with a click. Her clothes were ready to go, albeit two days early. Mentally she'd been ready to leave for weeks.

In a little more than forty-eight hours, she'd be on a beach in Florida soaking up the sun. Far from the cold and snow, she could forget about Dennis, the town that had started to take her for granted and the time of year that had lost its meaning somewhere between the stocking stuffers and the bargain hunters.

Her doorbell rang, and Bandit, her German shorthaired pointer, scrambled to his feet, bounding down the stairs at Greyhound speed, his tail a friendly whip against his hindquarters. To hedge his bets, he let out a few ferocious barks, but everyone in Riverbend knew Bandit had less guard dog in him than a stuffed frog.

She opened the door, expecting Mindy. "You can't talk me out—" The sentence died in her throat when she saw the tall, lean figure of C. J. Hamilton on her front porch. "It's you. Again."

"I'm not a man who gives up easily."

He had the kind of voice that sent a woman's pulse racing. Deep and thorough, he seemed to coat every syllable with a smoky accent.

Regardless of his voice or the way his dark hair swept one stubborn lock across his brow or how his jeans hugged his hips, she couldn't give him what he wanted. Christmas and Jessica Patterson were no longer operating hand in hand. "I'm sorry, Mr. Hamilton, but I thought I made this clear earlier. I will not be participating in any Christmas activities this year. Maybe I could refer you to one of my colleagues. There's even a network of Santa performers that are available for malls and private parties, if you—"

"It has to be here. And that means it has to be you."

"I'm leaving in two days. I won't even be here for Christmas, or even the Winterfest. I can't help you." She started to shut the door.

He was already digging in his back pocket, pulling out a leather billfold, flipping it open. His foot wedged in the door, preventing her from shutting him out. "I'll pay you. Name your price, Mrs. Patterson."

"I don't want your money."

"Name a charity you want me to support. A home for retired Santas you want me to build. Anything."

The laughter burst out of Jessica before she could stop it. "There's no such thing."

He answered her with a grin that took over his face, lighting his blue eyes, taking them from the color of a sluggish river to a sparkling ocean on a sunny day.

Oh, damn. She always had been a sucker for eyes like that. And especially a pair surrounded by deep lines of worry, shoulders hunched with the heaviness of sorrow and responsibility. Sarah Hamilton had, indeed, been through a lot, and so had her father, Jessica was sure.

She sighed. "Why don't you come in and have a cup of coffee? I won't be your Mrs. Claus—" at that she felt her face color, and saw him arch a brow, reading the slight innuendo, too "—but maybe I can help you find a solution to your…problem."

Some of the weight seemed to lift from him. "A cup of coffee would be great. Really great."

She invited him in, all the while wondering what she was thinking. She wanted to get away from reminders of Christmas, not open up her house to the season—or to a man who made her pulse race and clearly came attached to a whole set of problems.

C.J. stepped inside and glanced around her house. "Guess you weren't kidding about the no-Christmas thing. You don't have so much as a pine branch on your mantel."

"I didn't see the point in decorating if I was going to be out of town." Jessica chastised herself. The man could be a serial killer, a burglar or a Frosty thief. And she'd just broadcast that her house would be empty over the holidays.

Bandit had already warmed up to the newcomer, his wiry body pressed to C.J.'s jeans, tail wagging so hard it beat a pattern against Bandit's rump, his head under C.J.'s palm for a little TLC. C.J. had apparently passed Bandit's criminal background check.

"Bandit, leave him alone."

"He's fine," C.J. said, stroking Bandit's ears and sending the dog into hyper-puppy joy. "I work with a lot of animals on the set, too, and don't mind a dog. In fact, I'd have a dog myself if—"

He cut off the sentence. Jessica was intrigued—but not enough to ask. Her sole purpose of inviting C. J. Hamilton into the house was to make it clear she had no intentions of being part of a Christmas celebration—not the town's and not his.

The kitchen was right off the entryway, all in keeping with the small cottage-style house she had lived in since she'd married Dennis. Five rooms for two people. More than enough space.

Yet, somehow with C. J. Hamilton behind her as she led the way to the coffeepot, it seemed as if the house had shrunk, making her all too aware of the stranger in town.

"Cream or sugar?" she asked, crossing to the counter to pour coffee into a plain white mug. On any other year, she'd have the special Santa mugs out, with the dancing reindeer ringing the base. But not this year.

"Nothing, thanks." He accepted the mug from her, then took a seat at the table. "I bet your kids really love the toy store."

Jessica paused, took in a breath. A simple question, catching her off guard. She'd gone from pouring coffee to feeling as if she was going to cry.

It had to be the holiday that had her feeling so melancholy, so empty, so…

Alone.

"I don't have any children," she said, taking the opposite seat. She exhaled, erasing the subject from her memory, trying to refocus on C.J. and not on what might be lacking from her own life. The choices she had made. "Now, back to your Santa problem."

"I don't have a Santa problem, exactly. More a daughter problem. Sarah refuses to talk to me, and I'm sure she absolutely won't go back to California with me. I'd rather not drag her kicking and screaming. Even *I* know that's not the best way to build a new relationship." He threw up his hands. "I'm at a loss as to what to do."

"Did you ask LuAnn?" LuAnn Rivers was a

decent woman, good with kids and generous to a fault. A frequent shopper at Santa's Workshop Toys, she often brought a few of the children who went to her day care center along with her, buying them a toy because LuAnn knew money was tight at home or the child had had a bad day.

LuAnn had brought in Sarah more than once, which had Jessica tucking an extra special something into Sarah's bag—a new card game, a small stuffed animal—something that would cheer the girl. Jessica had never seen her smile and had often wondered how living with the chaotic Kiki must have been for Sarah.

Again a tug of sympathy pulled at Jessica's heart, urging her to stay in town. To believe in one more Christmas miracle.

No, she told herself. Those didn't happen anymore, and she was going to celebrate her Christmas on a beach this year, with a mai tai and a suntan.

"I did talk to LuAnn, but…" C.J. sighed and ran a hand through his hair. "It's really important that I find my own way to connect with Sarah, rather than relying on LuAnn. After all, LuAnn won't be with us in California, so I have to figure out how to do this."

"Well, there's plenty of time until Christmas and you can—"

"I don't have plenty of time," he said, cutting her off. "I have until December twenty-sixth before I have to head back to California for work. Soon as we get there, I'm packing to go to Colorado for a shoot, then the crew and I are off to—"

"Whoa, whoa. You can't just do that. You can't take that girl globe-trotting. She needs stability at a time like this," Jessica said, though she had never been a parent and hadn't any idea what the right thing was. "And especially not a world-wide tour for your—" she waved a hand, searching for the right words "—set stuff."

"For your information, this is not globe-trotting. I'm staying within the continental U.S.A. And that 'set stuff' is my job. If I don't keep that, Sarah won't have a roof over her head."

Steam rose in Jessica. How dare this man do something like that to Sarah? Then, just as quickly, guilt washed over her. Hadn't she herself called the child—

Oh, boy…a *brat?*

That alone was a sign that Jessica needed to get out of town, take a moment to remind herself why she'd gone into the toy business. Why she'd donned the Mrs. Claus outfit in the first place.

But at least she was acknowledging—okay, just to herself—but still, acknowledging that she'd rushed to judgment too fast, forgotten that Sarah was only six and was mostly a product of a mother who indulged her child's whims but provided about as much structure as a sand castle.

And now it turned out Sarah's father was just as bad.

"You came here, expecting me to help you create an instant bond with your daughter?" Jessica rose. "That's impossible. And selfish, if you ask me."

"I have more reasons than work bringing me back to California." C.J.'s eyes glittered with unspent frustration. "Reasons I don't care to share with you or anyone else in this town. All I want is a great Christmas for my daughter."

"And then what? You'll sort out the rest as you go along? Or keep flooding her with gifts?"

"I don't intend to do that." He glared at her, clearly angry she'd suggest such a thing. "I just need this particular gift-giving holiday to help me build a little camaraderie."

Typical, Jessica thought. Looking to first dump his problems on her, then expecting Jessica to provide a quick fix, a Band-Aid over the issues at heart with Sarah, so he could hurry and return to his life. Instead of dealing with the fallout from Kiki's unpredictable lifestyle.

He didn't appreciate the amazing gift he had been given, a gift Jessica would have done anything to have if things had been different. If only—

But she'd been right to be cautious, to accept the hand fate had dealt her. Look where she had ended up. A widow, alone. Raising a child and running a business would have meant sacrificing too much, and undoubtedly the child would have been the loser in that equation.

Now here came C. J. Hamilton, unwilling to see where his priorities should lie, when to Jessica the entire equation was simple arithmetic.

"You are exactly the kind of parent I'm trying to avoid this year. You can't buy and sell the affections of a child, like they're some kind of tech stock." She put her cup in the sink, then wheeled on him. "Invest *time*, Mr. Hamilton, not money, and you'll get better results."

He rose, facing her now, his frustration level clearly raised a few notches. "Listen, Mrs. Claus, you—"

"Patterson."

"You don't know my story, so quit trying to tell me the end. Twenty-four hours ago, I was a childless bachelor. Now I'm an instant father, and it's not going so well. I can't afford the time to hang around this dinky little town, hoping for a miracle breakthrough. I have to get back to work."

Jessica shook her head. Why had she ever found this man attractive? He was clearly all frosting and no substance. "That's the most selfish thing I've ever heard. A good father—"

"Don't tell me about good fathers," C.J. inter-rupted. "I know all about bad ones, and in my opinion, the best way to be a good one is to do the exact opposite of a bad father."

He didn't get it and she didn't have time to do pop psychology in her kitchen. Another wave of sympathy for Sarah ran through Jessica, urging her to stay in town, to go along with C.J.'s plan, if only for the sake of the child.

No. She would not be dissuaded. She'd pack up a box of wrapped toys and send them over to LuAnn's house, with a little note saying "Merry Christmas from Mrs. Claus." That way she avoided C. J. Hamilton and his crazy ideas about parenting but still brought a little special something to Sarah's holiday.

"I'm sorry. I can't help you." She took his coffee mug and put it in the sink, hoping he'd get the hint and just leave. "What you need, Mr. Hamilton, is a counselor, a mediator. Not me."

C.J. crossed to her, and she instantly became aware of his cologne. Slightly musky, with a hint of pine. He could have been a Christmas present himself—if only what was inside the box was as nice as the outside. "I need you and I need a miracle. Everyone I've talked to says you're the woman who can make that happen. What'll it take to convince you?"

She searched his gaze. "You being serious about being a father."

"I am serious."

"Then prove it. And hang around in Riverbend until *Sarah* is ready leave. Give her some time to grieve, to get used to you and to this new situation. *Then* take her to California. Give the girl a little stability before you yank her out of her world."

"I have a job—"

"Yes, you do. And it's called Father. Everything else takes a backseat." Oh, how she wanted to slug him, to shake him. Anything to make him see what a precious gift he'd been given and how he was blowing it already.

C.J. ran a hand through his hair again, something which only seemed to make him more attractive rather than less. He spun away from her, paced a few steps to the sink, then back. "You're right. I'll stay in Riverbend as long as I can, but on one condition." He approached her, his gaze holding a hint of a dare.

Desire tightened in Jessica's gut. A crazy feeling. She barely knew this man, had nothing in common with him, and five seconds ago had been on the brink of slugging him. Her attraction to him was nothing more than misplaced wanderlust.

"What do you mean, one condition?" she asked.

"You give something back."

"You can't bargain with me. I'm just giving you some advice."

He took another step closer. She inhaled the scent of his cologne again, watched his blue eyes. Wondered for a fleeting second what it would be like to kiss him. To have a man hold her again, love her, wrap her against his chest and make her feel safe. Fill that empty space in her bed, her heart, her life.

"This town needs you," C.J. said, "and I need you. I'll stay in Riverbend, but only if you do, too."

"I'm sorry," she said, backing up a step, away from those eyes, from their nearly hypnotic power that dimmed her common sense. She backed up until she hit the solid, sane, ordinary edge of the table. "I've already bought my ticket and I'm going, whether you or anyone else likes it."

"Didn't you just say that children should come first?"

"Well, yes, but I meant your own."

"From what I've heard, the people around here consider you a Christmas staple for their children. You give them the magic, that little extra something in the season. Without Mrs. Claus, they say, Christmas in Riverbend just won't be the same. So I'm asking you to hang up that bikini—" he paused long enough to take a breath, and she wondered if he was picturing her in said swimsuit, and what kind of image he was seeing "—and get out your red suit."

"If you can prove to me that there is one ounce of Christmas spirit left in this town, then—" she drew in a breath, knowing she was crazy for even letting this thought pass by her lips but letting it go anyway because some tiny part of her still had hope, in the children, the people of Riverbend "—then I'll *consider* staying."

"Thank you," C.J. said, the relief so clear she could almost see the weight of stress lift from his shoulders. "You've just—"

"Don't thank me yet." She held up a finger. "Because if I do stay, and that's a big if, there's one other thing Riverbend is going to need to make this Christmas perfect."

"If it's a reindeer, I have one on its way. If you want a twelve-foot tree, I'll call the arborist tomorrow. A giant—"

"No, none of those." Jessica drew in a breath. It was about time she quit the solo act. And besides, she had no doubt Mr. Get-Out-of-Town-Fast C. J. Hamilton would turn her down before the first snowflake fell on Riverbend. "What we really need in this town is a new Mr. Claus."

CHAPTER THREE

THE WIDE BLUE EYES regarded C.J. with suspicion. "Are you sure you know what you're doing?"

"Of course I do. Done it a hundred times." He picked up one of the—what the heck were they called anyway?—multicolored doohickeys on the table and hoped his daughter couldn't tell he was lying through his teeth.

Normally he wasn't a man given to lying, but then again, he wasn't normally a man used to being a father, either. He'd hoped to show up in town, get Jessica Patterson's help and then wham-bam, win over his daughter, thereby starting his new vocation off on the right foot, making the rest a piece of cake.

Clearly, he'd seen *Little Orphan Annie* one too many times.

Thus far, Jessica had refused to cooperate—okay maybe his idea had been a little crazy—and had thrown out her own crazy idea about him playing the big jolly Mr. to her Mrs., then herded him out of her house, telling him to go see his daughter.

Which he was doing. Unsuccessfully.

"I don't think you do," Sarah said, shaking her head. They were standing in the guest room LuAnn Rivers had set up as a temporary bedroom for Sarah—a bedroom which was quickly becoming permanent, mainly because his daughter still refused to go back to Kiki's apartment with C.J., clearly regarding him more as a kidnapper than a father. LuAnn had left the two of them here alone, saying she figured they would bond while Sarah got ready for a birthday party.

So far they'd bonded about as well as two pieces of wet tape.

Sarah had started talking to him—sort of—but only after a stern lecture from LuAnn, and only in monosyllabic words and eye rolls.

"I tied the bow on your dress for you, didn't I?" C.J. chanced a glance at the lopsided, twisted mess he'd made of the pink satin ribbon. Maybe not the best testament to his fashion skills. Good thing Sarah didn't have eyes at the back of her head. If she could see what he'd done to the sash, she'd never let him wield a brush near her curly locks.

Sarah gave him another dubious look. "I want Kiki to do it."

Kiki. Her mother. C.J. didn't find it in the least

surprising that Kiki wouldn't have wanted to be called Mommy.

"Kiki can't do it, honey," C.J. said, bending down to Sarah's level. As he did, the movement brought back another conversation, a memory of his own, slamming into him with a tidal force, nearly rocking him back on his heels. Someone telling him that he was about to be let down again—by the one person who was supposed to always be there. C.J. swiped the image away, focused again on Sarah's wide blue eyes. "She's…gone."

Sarah pouted, arms tight against her chest. "Everyone keeps telling me that. But I don't want her to be gone."

C.J. bit back a sigh. So far he was striking out as a father. He needed a "Dummies" manual. A crash course. A miracle. "Listen, Sarah, why don't I—"

"No! I don't *want* you to do it. *Kiki* does it right. You're a boy. Boys don't know how to do girl hair."

She had a point.

"We could wait for LuAnn to come back," C.J. said. Why had LuAnn left? What was she thinking? He had no clue how to handle this. And what if Sarah started crying? Or pitched a fit?

He was so far over his head, it was a wonder he could see daylight.

"She's at the hairdresser's." When Sarah said the word, it came out hare-testers. "That takes lots of time 'cuz they gotta put the colors in it and make it all curly again."

C.J. cursed himself for ever telling LuAnn he could do this on his own. Clearly, the visit to Jessica Patterson's house had left him on edge. With that feeling of unfinished business between them.

But she'd been right, damn it. He was hoping for the quick fix, so that he could just add Sarah into his life, like she was a potted plant.

It wasn't going to work that way. And the sooner C.J. figured out a way to muddle through this new "normal," the better. He'd start with the hair doo-hickeys and move forward from there.

Sarah glared at him. "I'm gonna be late. And then Cassidy will never talk to me again 'cuz I missed her party and it's all your fault. And Kiki's." She plopped onto her bed and turned away. One of her dozen stuffed unicorns fell off the twin and tumbled to the floor, little sparkles dusting the dark-blue carpet.

C.J. fumbled for the brush, but the doohickey ponytail things caught on his fingers, the little round balls click-clacking together, giving him an extra quartet of thumbs. The brush slipped from his grasp and fell to the floor, bonking Mr. Unicorn on the head.

He looked at Sarah, hoping she would laugh at his hapless attempt. He even held up his multicolored thumbs. She ignored him, instead bending to pick up the brush and then putting it on her nightstand. She gave him an I-told-you-so sigh and retreated to her pillows again.

Beside him, he heard a sniffle, then a catch, then a full-out sob. Oh, damn. Now she was crying. C.J. hadn't the foggiest idea what to do.

Give him a knot in a piece of wood, and he could coax the best side out of the hard oak. Throw him together with an ego-driven director, a penny-pinching producer and a movie star terrified the lighting might show her true age and latest face-lift, and he'd find a way to make everyone happy with a slight shifting of a plant here, a building there, a wall here. Put a complicated set design in front him with an insane deadline, and he'd thrive under the pressure, rise to the challenge, and never break a sweat, while his crew would fret and pace, sure the impossible could not be accomplished.

But a crying first-grader?

There wasn't any course in film school for that. And nothing he'd seen in the books he'd read in the past few days to cover ponytails, birthday party emergencies and clueless dads.

Should he get her a tissue? Tell her to stop? Call for backup?

LuAnn was gone, probably for hours. That left one other female solution.

"I know who can do this hair stuff, Sarah," C.J.

said. "And she'll probably throw in a Slinky for all
your trouble, too."

Sarah rolled over, and C.J. could see the stain of
tears running down her cheeks, doubling his guilt
and feelings of inadequacy. Oh, man, he really
needed a better parenting manual. "Who?"

Another tear brimmed in the corner of Sarah's
eye, and C.J. reached forward, plucked tissues one-
two-three-four from the box on her nightstand and
handed them to her in a big wad. "You know the toy
shop downtown? The one owned by—"

"Mrs. Claus?"

"How do you know that?"

Sarah rolled her eyes at him. "*Everyone* knows
that, even though it's s'pposed to be a secret, 'cuz
she works at Santa's toy store. Only she doesn't have
her suit on." Sarah's eyes brightened, then dimmed.
She looked down at the ball of white in her palms
and started shredding the paper. "Only I hear she
won't be Mrs. Claus this year, 'cuz she's going to
Florida or something. Maybe she doesn't like kids
anymore."

"Oh, no, she likes kids. *Loves* 'em. She told me
so." She hadn't said any such thing, but heck, C.J.
was already on a lying streak, might as well keep it
up. Besides, the mention of Jessica—Mrs. Claus—
seemed to have opened up a direct line to Sarah's
voice box, increasing C.J.'s reasons for getting the

woman involved. He handed Sarah more tissues, hoping it would head off any subsequent tears. "And she's really good at doing hair, too."

Liar, liar.

"She can do my hair 'fore I have to go to Cassidy's party?"

"Certainly." *If she hasn't left for her flight yet. If she's still talking to me. If a hundred other ifs haven't gone wrong.* He put out his hand, but Sarah didn't take it. "Do you want to see if she can fix your hair?"

"Okay." Sarah still looked unconvinced, but she slipped down off her bed and grabbed her party shoes off the floor, dropping the tissues into a puffy white pile in their place.

She did a half turn, then caught her reflection in the mirror that hung over her dresser. She put one hand on her hip and cast another I-told-you-so glance at her newly minted father. "I sure hope Mrs. Claus knows how to tie a bow, too, 'cuz you're making a mess of things."

Sarah didn't how right she was.

C. J. Hamilton was on her doorstep for the second time in the space of a day. Jessica didn't know whether to be flattered or to take out a restraining order.

She glanced at her suitcase, sitting beside the door. Soon enough she'd be on her way, far from

Riverbend. Christmas and all the memories that holiday conjured would be out of mind and out of sight.

Less than forty-eight hours. That was all, and she'd be gone. She'd purposely booked the trip for the night of the Winterfest, to give her an excuse to miss the event and get out of her Mrs. Claus duties. And yet, here was C. J. Hamilton like a rebounding ball, determined to get her into that silly red suit.

"Mr. Hamilton," she said as she pulled open the door. "Again."

"I have a problem." He held up his hand, gaily decorated with ponytail holders, then gestured toward Sarah, who Jessica now noticed was standing next to him, arms crossed over her chest, face screwed up in disapproval. Her hair was a jumble of curls on her head, her dress a crinkled mess, the bow haphazardly tied and tilted at an odd angle. The gift in her hands had been wrapped either by C.J. himself or by a barrel of monkeys.

Jessica bit back a laugh. "I can see that."

"He tried to help me," Sarah said, her tone grumpy, face sullen. "He's not very good at it."

Jessica bent down, a burst of sympathy running through her for the motherless girl. How she wanted to just pull Sarah into her arms and fill her with cookies and hugs. But Sarah wasn't her daughter and Jessica reminded herself to keep her distance, guard her emotions. "I can see that," she repeated, softly, just for Sarah.

"Hey, I'm new at this." C.J. took Jessica's hand and dumped the ponytail holders into her palm. "Here. You do it."

Jessica stared at the multicolored elastics with their jaunty rainbow of balls. He expected her to just know how to do this? "What about LuAnn?"

"She had an appointment. And Sarah has a birthday party to get to."

Jessica thought a second. "Cassidy Rendell's seventh birthday, am I right?"

"Yeah," Sarah said, surprise arching her brows. "How'd you know?" Her expression perked up when Bandit wriggled his body between them and inserted a friendly doggy nose against her hip.

Jessica put a finger beside her nose, the familiar gesture she and Dennis had used to imply a Santa-only secret. Only she wasn't playing Mrs. Claus this year. So she couldn't very well pretend she had any secrets or magic. She lowered her hand and tried to ignore the whisper of wistfulness that ran through her. "Mrs. Klein and Tammy were in the store yesterday, talking about it," she said, naming one of the other first-graders in Sarah and Cassidy's class.

"Did they buy her a doctor Barbie? 'Cuz that's what I got her and I told Cassidy nobody else better bring one, 'cuz I want my present to be the most special one."

"No, they didn't. I think your gift—" she gestured toward the badly taped and wrapped box, then looked at C.J., who gave her another what-do-I-know, hands-up gesture "—is going to be perfect."

Sarah beamed and gave Bandit extra pats.

"I told Sarah you'd know how to do her hair. Tie her bow. That kind of girl stuff."

"Because I'm a girl, is that it? I must come prewired to do all this?"

He nodded. "Yeah."

She grabbed his palm and put the ponytails back into his grasp. "I hate to disappoint you, Mr. Hamilton, but my personal résumé doesn't include small children."

"But you're ah, you know, *her*," C.J. said, the implied meaning, that Santa's wife should know all things child related. "You own a toy store. You work with small children every day."

"That doesn't mean I know how to—" She cut off her words when she noticed Sarah watching the entire exchange. "I thought someone said something about not wanting any help?"

"I didn't know that meant being Bill Blass and Vidal Sassoon at the same time." He gestured to Sarah's mess of a bow and unkempt hair. "Will you please help me?"

She should say no. Be firm with C. J. Hamilton, wish him well and get back to—

To what? She had nothing to occupy her evening. She could go back to the toy shop, put in a few more hours, but she had a capable staff running the operation—a staff that would be surprised to see the boss back right after she'd left for the day.

There was no one waiting for her in the kitchen, no one expecting a dinner, a conversation by the fireplace. Nothing but an empty house, a dog whose affections were easily swayed and a packed suitcase.

And here was a child, a motherless child, who needed help.

Jessica bent down to Sarah's level. The little girl's face was tearstained, her eyes red rimmed. Whatever temper tantrums Sarah might have pitched in the toy store before were forgotten, as Jessica's heart opened up to this near-orphaned girl who just wanted to get to a party, see her friends and pretend her upside-down life was normal.

That Jessica could understand. And was powerless to close her door against. "Why don't you come in," she said, to Sarah and then to C.J. "And we'll see what we can do about getting you ready for Cassidy's party."

Fifteen minutes later, Jessica had managed to corral Sarah's curly locks into two neat ponytails, then straighten the bow on her dress. "Thank you," Sarah said, spinning on the kitchen floor, admiring what she could see of her sash from over her shoulder. "I was starting to get a little worried, there."

"You were?" Jessica said, biting back laughter at the nearly adult tone in Sarah's voice. "Why?"

Sarah paused in her twirling and leaned to whisper in Jessica's ear. "Because he—" at that, she thumbed toward C.J. "—doesn't know what he's doing."

Jessica bit back another laugh, and saw C.J. doing the same. "I think he'll figure it out as you two go along, don't you?"

Sarah shrugged. "Maybe." She grabbed her present off the table and clutched it to her chest, like a shield, as if she was trying to keep her distance. To keep from warming up to this stranger who was her father. "Can I go to my party now?"

"Sure, sure," C.J. said. "Cassidy's house, right?" He fished his keys out of his pocket but stayed where he was in the kitchen, another lost, blank look on his face.

A second wave of sympathy ran through Jessica. At this rate, she'd be writing greeting cards for the man. She needed to quit being such a softie. "Do you know where Cassidy lives?"

"I didn't think to ask," C.J. said. "I guess I thought…"

"A six-year-old could give you directions?"

"I know where Cassidy lives," Sarah put in. "She's got a big green house and a small blue car and she has a flag in her yard. And a dog named Boo and a cat named Wink. And her street is really pretty, and it has this big yellow house next door that looks kinda scary but isn't 'cuz I trick-or-treated there one time and the lady was nice and gave me a Snickers. A big one, too. Not those baby candies."

C.J. rocked back on his heels. "Wow, that's more than I've heard in the last twenty-four hours."

"That's 'cuz I like talking to her." Sarah pointed at Jessica. "'Cuz she's Mrs. Santa and she gave me an extra toy one time 'cuz I was sad." Sarah looked at Jessica. "Don't worry. I won't tell anybody 'bout who you are. I guessed it all by myself, even though Kylie said she knew before I did."

"Oh, I'm not Mrs. Claus," Jessica replied, telling Sarah the same thing she'd told hundreds of kids over the years. They all tried to guess, and she and Dennis had always denied their identities, to keep up the charade. "The real Mrs. Claus lives at the North Pole with Santa."

"Uh-huh," Sarah said, grinning, and not believing a word.

"I know where Cassidy lives," Jessica said to C.J., changing the subject. "We can take my car and I can drive, if you want."

"Can I ride up front?" Sarah asked.

"I don't think that's a good idea," C.J. said. "You're still little and the safest place to be is in the back seat." At Jessica's curious glance, he grinned. "I've been reading. Picked up a bunch of those parenting magazines and books at the bookstore after I, ah, got the call. I know more about natural childbirth than any man wants to know."

"I'll keep that in mind," Jessica said, laughing, and wondering what it was about this man and this child that had turned her mood sunny side up.

And had her reconsidering the very escape plan she'd put such stock in this morning.

A half hour later Sarah was overdosing on chocolate cake at Cassidy's house, and C.J. was pulling up in front of Jessica's house, after driving her back home. In the end, they'd opted to take his truck, a good thing because a mild winter storm started up as soon as they left the house.

Already he was wishing the night didn't have to end, that he could find a way to extend the moment between them. Because he'd found himself enjoying it more than he'd expected. "Thanks," he said.

Yeah, there was a real time waster, C.J.

"You're welcome." A light snow had started up, dusting the windshield with white powder, coating the streets with a fine sheen. The moonlight hazed through the storm, dropping a veil over the sky. Several houses had their Christmas lights burning, providing a twinkling accent to the snow. Coupled with the Christmas carols playing softly on the truck's stereo, it all had that special holiday glitter, whispering that something wonderful was on its way.

For a second C.J. watched the snow fall, transfixed, wrapped in the spell. Believing in that something wonderful, too.

Until the click of the door handle jerked him back to reality. "Wait," C.J. said to Jessica. "Don't go, not yet."

"I have…" She glanced at the house, then back at him. "I have a minute."

Where to begin to tell her how grateful he was for her help? She'd smoothed things over with Sarah, so well his daughter had run out of the truck with a wave and a smile, no longer the sullen child who'd refused to look at him. Jessica had done so much more than just give him tips on "girl hair" as she'd worked the ponytails into Sarah's hair, she'd given him hope.

Hope that if he could figure out ponytails, maybe he could get the harder parts under control, too.

"Thank you," C.J. said. "You've helped me tonight, more than you know."

"It was nothing."

"No, it helped Sarah and me turn a corner." He

knew, though, that all of this was probably a temporary reprieve. Soon he'd be on his own. Which meant
he still needed that miracle. "If I can prove to you
there is Christmas spirit left in this town, will you
stay and help me make this a holiday that Sarah will
never forget?"

She shifted in her seat to face him, her features
delicately lit by the streetlight above, giving her an
almost ethereal presence. "*You're* going to do that in
less than two days? The same man who couldn't get
his daughter's hair into two ponytails?"

"Hey, those things are tougher than they look."

"I appreciate your earnestness, Mr. Hamilton, but
my plane ticket is bought."

"Change it. What'll it cost you, seventy-five
bucks to change the date? Leave on December
twenty-sixth or New Year's Eve, I don't care. Just
don't leave before Sarah has a perfect Christmas."

"Why is this so important to you?"

"Because I'm her father." There were more
reasons than that, but he didn't share them. There
were simply things he didn't tell other people, doors
he didn't open. Even for himself.

Yet he could see the lingering doubts in Jessica's
face, and knew he had to offer at least a partial ex-
planation. "I lived my life being constantly reminded
that I was the result of someone else's one-night-in-
a-back-seat mistake. I refuse to let Sarah feel that

she's the same, just because things didn't work out between Kiki and me, and because she didn't tell me I was Sarah's real father. Kiki was…" He paused, searching for the right word.

"Unconventional."

"Exactly. And I may not have any idea how to tie a bow or do a braid, but I do know that I won't let my child grow up feeling the same way I did. That's why it's so important for me to let her know that I care, that she's important. And the best way I can see to do that is by giving her a holiday she'll never forget."

"And in order to do that you have to have me? Why?"

He grinned. "What's Christmas without Santa and Mrs. Claus?"

But Jessica didn't reflect his smile. "There is no more Santa. He died two years ago."

"I'm sorry," C.J. said, and he was, genuinely sorry for her. It explained a lot, he realized. Especially why she wanted to avoid the holiday.

She sighed. "Ever since my husband died, Christmas hasn't been the same. As much as I'd like to help you, I can't. I just don't believe in the holiday like I used to." Before he could stop her, she turned and got out of the truck.

C.J. rushed after her, catching up to her on the brick walkway. "Jessica, wait, please." He caught her arm and she slid a bit on the snow, losing her balance on the slippery stuff, falling into his arms.

She landed against his chest, her face upturned, all green eyes and blond hair and something more. Something he hadn't seen or had in his life in a very long time.

Something he'd given up hope on thinking he could ever find—or have.

She was warm against him, her body curving perfectly to his. "Sorry," C.J. said, his voice gruff and rough against his throat. "I made you lose your footing."

"Yeah." Her gaze lingered on his a moment longer, before she righted herself. "Well, good night. I hope Sarah has a nice time at the party."

"What about you?" Curiosity to know more, to find out what made this woman tick, grew inside him. "What will *you* be doing tonight, Jessica?" He loved the way her name slid off his tongue, almost like candy.

A bittersweet smile crossed her lips and it was all C.J. could do to keep from hauling her to him again, just to erase that melancholy. "Same thing I always do. Same thing I've done for the past two years. A cup of tea, a little reading, in bed by ten."

"And what would you do if someone changed your routine?" He took a step closer, mesmerized by her eyes, the falling snow, the season that seemed to wrap around them, magical in its difference from the California sun that normally greeted his days.

"I don't…" She paused, tried again. "I like to know what's coming at the end of the day. It makes it easier."

Easier for what? he wanted to ask but didn't. Instead he found himself watching her lips, the tendrils of air that escaped her mouth, frosted by the cold. "And then here I came along and made things harder?"

She nodded, her gaze on his, the only sound around them the soft rustling of leaves being weighed down by the snow, coming heavier now, thicker. Maybe it was the snow. Maybe it was the connection he'd felt when they'd touched. Maybe it was just him being incredibly selfish.

C.J. didn't know and didn't care. "I'm sorry," he said again.

"For what?"

"I'm about to make things twice as difficult." Before he could think twice, C.J. leaned forward and kissed her holly-red lips, bringing Jessica against him.

She tasted of coffee and snow, of long nights by the fire, tucked beneath a blanket. She was sweet in his arms, soft wherever he was hard, and easy against him. Her arms went around him, and for one sweet moment C. J. Hamilton felt as if he'd come home.

Their kiss was too short, too brief, nearly chaste.

And yet it touched something in him that lay deep inside, as quiet as this town. It was a kiss that held the same whispered promise as the snow.

That something wonderful was on its way—if only the right flakes could fall at the right time.

"That probably wasn't the wisest thing to do." Jessica's voice shook a little on the last syllable, the only betrayal that she had been as moved by the moment as he.

"No, it wasn't," C.J. agreed, reminding himself that his priority right now was his daughter. Kisses—and what they might hold down the road—would have to wait. "But it did prove one thing."

"What's that?"

"That a little something unexpected can sometimes be very, very nice."

She shook her head. "Or just one more reason to leave town. Before something like that happens again."

C.J. watched Jessica Patterson turn away, climb her walkway and go into her house. The light in the hallway stayed on for a moment, then went off, effectively shutting him out.

She needed a Christmas miracle. And he intended to give her one.

Even if he had to manufacture it himself.

CHAPTER FOUR

"HOW'S COME you're not dressed in your Mrs. Santa outfit?"

Sarah Hamilton sat in Jessica's shop, swinging her legs back and forth on a chair just a tad too tall for her. It was another twenty minutes or so until the store officially opened for the day, and Sarah had spent the last five minutes shooting questions at Jessica, one right after the other, like a three-foot-tall machine gun.

When Jessica arrived at work, C.J. had been at the door, asking if he could drop the girl off and if Jessica could watch his daughter for just a few minutes while he ran an errand he wouldn't name. School was already out for winter break, LuAnn was at a doctor's appointment, and he was in a pinch. When she'd asked what his errand was, he'd only smiled, distracting her so much she'd barely remembered what favor he'd asked. Before Jessica could get out the words, "I'm not a babysitting service," he was gone and Sarah had turned into a mini question dispenser.

Jessica peeked over the pile of stuffed white bears, hoping Sarah might have gotten interested in the coloring books and crayons on the round table set up as a "busy center" in the center of the store, so parents could shop while their kids stayed occupied.

Apparently all kids but Sarah Hamilton.

The inquisitive girl didn't have so much as a burnt sienna in her hands, nary a streak of color on the white pages before her. "How's come?" she asked again.

"I didn't want to wear the suit today." Jessica had no intentions of explaining her entire life story to a six-year-old.

Sarah considered that. She reached for a magenta crayon, picked it up, put it back down again without even streaking the page. Jessica bit back a sigh.

"How's come you don't have your tree up?" Sarah asked. "It's Christmas, you know."

Jessica glanced at the corner of the store where her seven-foot Christmas tree normally stood.

Every year she'd gone down to the Methodist Church's tree lot, chosen the best Scotch pine, then hauled it back to the store and decorated it herself from top to bottom—the entire works, from blinking lights to tinsel, all the way to a twirling star on the top.

Then she'd do the whole thing all over again for the tree at home, sometimes setting up two—one in the living room, one in the front room, facing the bay windows that looked out over the street. Dennis, who loved all things Christmas, hadn't had the patience for the lights, the ornaments and the several-hour tree process. He'd always dropped that particular chore into Jessica's lap, preferring to put the carols on the stereo and putter around in the back, working on the store's books or wrapping gifts, rather than throw tinsel onto pine.

So, she'd hummed "Frosty" and set her lights at-winkling alone, every single year—

Every year but this one. This year, the days had seemed to get away from her, and then, once she'd booked the trip to the tropics, buying and decorat-ing a tree had seemed almost silly. A waste of time and money.

Jessica returned her gaze to the center table and realized Sarah was still waiting for her answer. "Because I didn't have time to get it decorated."

"I could help you." Sarah pushed back her chair and ran over to the empty corner, twirling in the space, as if her bright-green-plaid skirt could take the place of the tree. "A tree would look so, so pretty here, too. And I could climb on a ladder and hang the ornaments and string the lights up and even plug 'em in and test 'em. I'd be real careful, too, not to 'lectrocute myself 'cuz if I went to the hospital, that'd be bad. And then C.J. would get really mad, I think." She brightened again, still spinning. "But if I was *really* careful, could I help? Could I?"

"Thank you for offering, Sarah, but—"

"That's okay, I guess." The girl's face fell. "Kiki never liked Christmas trees. She said the needles were messy. And the lights gave her a headache. So we never had a tree."

Jessica knelt before Sarah, catching the miniature human spinning top. "Never?"

Sarah shook her head. "I like Christmas trees. But I never told Kiki, 'cuz she didn't like 'em and I didn't want her to get mad. Or get a headache. But she did fun things, like hide the presents under the bed and it was kinda cool, 'cept one time when LuAnn's cat snuck in our 'partment and chewed on all the wrappin' paper. That's how I knew I was gettin' a Twister game last year." Sarah sighed. "But I still missed havin' a tree. 'Cuz they're real sparkly."

Jessica looked at the empty corner, which had seemed so spacious five minutes ago and now just looked bare…almost lonely.

Then she glanced again at the little girl, who had gone back to twirling, her arms outstretched, finger-tips touching the edge of her skirt as it lifted with the movement, touching the green-tipped hem. She spun and spun, creating magic of her own.

To replace the magic she'd never had.

Mindy had been right, Jessica thought, seeing her undecorated shop for the first time. The store had the Santa theme, but it lacked the usual Christmas touches Jessica always added, the extra oomph she'd loved giving every space at Christmas, all to make up for the barren spaces she'd had as a child. The empty rooms, empty belly, empty fireplace, all markers of an even emptier bank account. Her father had worked hard—when he had worked—and her mother had done her best, with what little she'd had.

It was part of what Jessica had loved about Dennis. His enthusiasm for giving. For spreading joy and gifts to all the children of the town, especially those who had so little. And now she had a child before her who was missing out on one of the simplest joys of the holiday.

A tree.

It *was* Christmas, after all. The busiest shopping season of the year. A tree was almost a necessity in a toy store. Part of getting shoppers in the holiday mood. And if it helped one little girl find a bit of something she'd never had…

How hard would it be to add some greenery?

"Putting up a Christmas tree is an awful lot of work," Jessica began, unable to tear her gaze away from Sarah's twirling, the wistful look in the young girl's eyes, "and *if* we're going to do this, I'll need you to—"

"Yes! Yes! I will!" Sarah stopped spinning and leaped up and down. "And when we're done, can I put the star on top? Please? Pretty, pretty please?"

The bell over the door jingled, ushering in several customers and two of the extra helpers Jessica had hired for the Christmas season, as well as Mindy, who'd promised to come by and help for the morning rush, too. Jessica suspected Mindy's impromptu offer to help ring up sales was more a last-ditch attempt to convince Jessica not to get on that plane tomorrow.

"Hey, Jessica," Mindy said, whisking some snow off her hair as she came inside. "I think it'll be a busy day here today. I heard a lot of the moms in the parking lot at the YMCA making plans to stop over here after they finished dropping off their kids at the winter sports program."

"Great." The two of them started walking toward the back room, with Sarah running alongside Jessica, still bouncing up and down with every step.

"Are we gonna go now, Mrs. Claus? Are we? Are we?"

"Sarah, I told you I'm not Mrs. Claus."

"Oops," Sarah said, with a smile. "I meant, Mrs. Patterson."

"Going somewhere?" Mindy asked.

"I promised Sarah I'd take her to buy a Christmas tree for the store."

Mindy gave her a knowing look. "I thought you weren't putting up the tree this year."

"I changed my mind." Jessica gestured toward Sarah. "Or rather, someone changed it for me."

"Needing a little extra Christmas spirit, are we?"

"Just a little."

Mindy smiled. "Good. She's not the only one at that."

In the back room of the shop, Mindy hung up her coat, Sarah wriggled into hers and Jessica slid her own on, too. "I'm still leaving tomorrow."

"I didn't say anything," Mindy replied.

"I know what you're thinking and I know why you volunteered to help ring up sales. You're hoping you can talk me out of this vacation."

Mindy put a hand to her chest and feigned horror. "Who? Me? Try to talk you out of an incredibly stupid decision?"

Jessica laughed. "My bags are packed, my ticket's bought and I am leaving no matter what."

Sarah looked up at her. "How can you go away? You're *Mrs. Claus.* Aren't you supposed to put the angel on the tree at the winter thing? And who's going to listen to my Christmas list? C.J. said you were going to come. Aren't you?"

Mindy gave her a smile. "Yes, aren't you?"

Jessica bent down to Sarah's level. "There will be plenty of other people to do all those things, I'm sure. I have to take a trip this year."

"You're *leaving?*" Sarah sounded betrayed.

Jessica halted midstep, stunned. She thought of Sarah's perspective. Just having lost her mother. Being introduced to a brand-new father. A whole lot of scary changes all at once. No wonder Sarah saw it that way.

Jessica knew scary. Remembered it well from her childhood and immediately regretted that Sarah had overheard the conversation with Mindy. The last thing this child needed was more upheaval.

"The only place I'm going right now is to buy a Christmas tree," Jessica said, changing the subject and reaching forward to button the little girl's coat. "And for that, I need a helper."

"I can be a helper."

"Good." She plopped the girl's red cap on her head, tugged it down over her ears, then rose. "Go get your boots. They're by the door. I'll be out in a second."

With a grin and a nod, Sarah dashed out the door to do as she was told.

"Putting up a tree sounds a lot like celebrating Christmas to me," Mindy said. "For someone who is trying to avoid the holiday, you seem to be running smack-dab into it."

"One little tree is nothing more than that. A tree.

And I'm only doing it because Sarah has never had a Christmas tree before. Kiki told Sarah they gave her a headache."

The two of them exited the back room. Mindy paused after shutting the door and gave Jessica a smile. "I know you, Jessica. I know how you feel about Christmas trees. And kids. Mark my words. Before the last piece of tinsel is hung, you'll be changing that plane ticket."

Jessica dismissed Mindy's words as she headed down Main Street with Sarah in tow. She was only buying the tree to give one little girl a bit of pine-scented magic.

If that was so, then why did she find herself humming a Christmas carol under her breath? What was with the smile that suddenly appeared on her face? And why was she so excited about picking out a silly tree?

They reached the busy corner of Main and Reed. The light changed, the walk signal flashed. "Ready, Sarah?"

The little girl beamed. Jessica wondered how she could have ever thought this child was a brat. "Abso-toot-ly."

Jessica laughed. "Then let's walk on down to the corner and pick out the fattest, greenest, tallest tree we can find." She put out her hand.

Sarah hesitated, then put her palm into Jessica's, her small hand delicate and fragile. She looked up, a question on her lips that she didn't ask, then followed along, her fingers curling into Jessica's with a shy grip that tightened with every step.

Something tugged at Jessica's heart, causing her eyes to sting and her step to falter. It had to be the winter wind, the cold air skating under her coat.

Not the feeling of Sarah's hand in hers and the momentary thought of what could have been, if only—

"Hey, where are you off to?"

Jessica turned to see C. J. Hamilton standing on the sidewalk, a grin on his face and a whole bunch of boxes stacked in the back of his truck. Some marked Fragile, others marked Special Delivery. He'd been up to something, that much was clear.

"We're going to get a tree," Sarah said. "A *Christmas* tree. Do you wanna come?"

For a moment Jessica wanted him to say no. Then she wanted him to say yes. Then she didn't want to hear his answer, she just wanted to keep on walking and not have to deal with C.J. or the way looking at him reminded her—in living Technicolor and broad, sweeping sunshine—of how it felt to kiss him last night.

Or rather, how it felt when *he* kissed *her.*

And how many times the thought of her kissing

him back had crossed her mind before she'd finally fallen asleep.

"Picking out a Christmas tree, huh?" he said. "I have a whole lot to do today, to get this town ready for one heck of a Winterfest tomorrow night," with that, he gave Jessica a wink, "but I think I can fit in a tree-picking with two beautiful girls."

"You think I'm boo-ti-fool?" Sarah asked, slipping her hand into C.J.'s, and adding him to her other flank.

"Of course I do."

"And you think Jessica's boo-ti-fool, too?"

He caught Jessica's eye over Sarah's head, and suddenly she no longer felt the cold. Heck, she no longer felt her toes or anything else. Just the searing power of those blue eyes, and the way his voice seemed to touch a part of her she'd thought had died a long time ago. "Yes. Very much so."

"Good. Then we have to find a boo-ti-ful tree, too."

And off they went, looking more like the trio in the *Wizard of Oz* than anything else, Jessica thought. But if anyone in Riverbend found the three of them an odd grouping, they didn't say a word. At the corner, the church lot had plenty of trees left, and Sarah was soon darting from tree to tree, pronouncing one after another perfect and boo-ti-ful.

"She's having a blast," Jessica said to C.J. "I can't imagine never having a Christmas tree."

"Sarah's never had a tree before?"

The surprise in his voice reminded her of how little he knew about his daughter. What an absent father he had been. Yet another reason not to get involved with this man. He'd said he had no idea that he had a child, but she had to wonder, had he just walked away from Kiki or ignored her attempts to let him know she was pregnant?

There were two sides to every story, and she wondered about the side C.J. was leaving out.

Still, Sarah deserved and needed a Christmas tree. And if Jessica could help the little girl get that much at least before she left for Miami, then she'd leave feeling better. So she explained to C.J. what Sarah had told her earlier.

"I had no idea," C.J. said. "I mean, Kiki wasn't exactly traditional, but I thought she at least celebrated Christmas."

"Apparently not. At least not like everyone else."

C.J. watched his little girl run among the trees, her face bright, eyes wide. Jessica read the emotions running across C.J.'s face like a river rushing over rocks.

Anger yielding to regret, then that was swept away by a tender determination. She took back her earlier thoughts about him, replacing them with newfound respect for his parenting efforts. He slipped his hand into Jessica's. "It seems we have a mission, then."

No man had touched her since her husband died and here C.J. had done it twice. C.J.'s palm was broad and firm, his grip warm and so large, so strong. A thrill ran up her arm, then through her body. For a second she couldn't think, couldn't breathe.

A simple thing, a touch like that, and yet how she had missed it. And not even known she'd missed it until C.J. had taken her hand, kissed her.

Woken her up, like the sun cresting over the horizon and brightening a sleeping landscape. Hunger roared to life inside her for more of this. More of him.

"A…a mission?" she managed.

"To find the biggest damned tree on this lot," he said, grinning, clearly excited by the prospect. His enthusiasm spread to her. "No, not just one, because that one is for your store, right?"

She nodded, her gaze stealing to their clasped palms. As he talked, his grip on hers tightened, but he seemed to barely notice.

But she noticed. She noticed every ounce of his touch.

"Three," C.J. said with finality. "Three trees, that's how many we need."

"Three?" Had she heard him right? "Why three?"

"One for your store. One for Sarah's living room and one for yours."

"But, but I won't be there. I'm leaving."

He took her hand, raised it to his lips and pressed a kiss to the back of her hand. Even through the leather of her glove, she could feel the warmth of his breath. "No, you're not going to leave. Because I am going to do everything I can to convince you to stay."

"C.J.—"

"Can I help you folks?" Earl Klein sauntered over to them, his brown plaid hunting cap pulled low on his head, the ear flaps tipped up, flopping like puppy ears as he walked. He had his Carhartt overalls on, making him look like a big brown Pillsbury Doughboy. "Oh, Mrs. Patterson! I was wondering when you were coming down for your tree this year. I have a great one set aside for you."

"Earl, thank you, but I'm not planning on getting a tree."

"Not getting a tree!" Earl dug a finger into his ear canal. "I better get down to the doc, because I think my hearing is going."

"I'm serious, Mr. Klein. I'm only getting a tree for the store this year."

Earl looked at C.J., then down at Sarah. "She's pulling my leg, isn't she? Trying to pull some wool over old Earl." Then he glanced back up at Jessica. "Very funny there, Mrs. Patterson. Now come see this gorgeous Scotch pine—" He started walking away.

"Mr. Klein, I'm serious."

Earl stopped dead in his tracks. "I'm going to pretend I didn't hear that because you are *Mrs. Claus,*" he whispered the last two words so Sarah couldn't hear, "and that means you can't go without a tree in your house." He gave her a finger wag. "Now you can put this tree in your kitchen and use it to hang your dish towels on for all I care, but I can't, in good conscience, let you leave my lot, without knowing you, of all people, is setting right."

"Exactly my thinking, Mr. Klein," C.J. agreed.

"Let me just pay for the store's tree," Jessica said, hoping if she ignored the argument Earl would let it go, and reached for her wallet.

Earl waved her off. "No charge. You do enough for this town, ma'am. 'Bout time this town did something for you."

"But, Mr. Klein, I always support the church's tree sale."

"I know." He glanced at C.J., and the two men exchanged a smile. Jessica shot C.J. a suspicious look. "And now *we're* supporting *you.*" Before she could say anything else, Earl waved an arm toward the back of the lot. "Now, let me show you your tree, and then you can tell me if you don't want it."

"What did you do?" she asked C.J. as the three of them navigated through a maze of pine, down a carpet of thick green needles, to a stand of trees set up around the corner and behind the main tree lot.

"Nothing. Nothing at all."

But the dimple in his smile belied every word.

"Your tree, Mrs. Claus," Earl whispered the last, then stepped back and gestured to a thick, lush, bright-green, seven-foot-tall Scotch pine, perfectly shaped and exactly the right size for the store's corner.

"It's perfect!" Sarah said. She ran to the tree, halting just before it, then flung out her arms—

And gave the tree a hug.

"I'd say that one's sold," C.J. said. "Can we get two more just like it?"

"One more," Jessica corrected.

"Two," C.J. overrode.

"One."

Earl looked from C.J. to Jessica. "Ain't she pretty? Didn't I tell you?"

Sarah quit hugging the tree and turned around. "Are we getting three trees? Really getting three?"

Her voice was so filled with wonder and excitement, that it evoked a memory in Jessica's heart, and when Jessica opened her mouth to say "no," the word somehow got twisted around in her throat and came out… "Yes. Three trees it is."

C.J. grinned and gave Jessica's hand a squeeze. "What's the worst that can happen? You come home and have to vacuum up a few pine needles?"

She met his charismatic blue eyes—as rich and deep as the needles on the tree before her—got wrapped up in his charming smile again, and knew there were far worse things already afoot than pine needles falling on her living room carpet.

CHAPTER FIVE

THE THREE OF THEM sat in a booth at a little deli next to the Methodist Church in a scene so normal, so ordinary, C.J. would have thought he was on the set of *Leave It to Beaver,* except for the feel of the laminate tabletop beneath his palms and the scent of bacon in the air. Not to mention what would undoubtedly be some damned good blueberry pancakes, if the number of orders surrounding them was any indication.

This was how regular people lived. A life C.J. had never known, only glimpsed in windows, seen on the sets he built. And yet it was the exact life he wanted to give Sarah, if only he could figure out how.

"I'm bored," Sarah said, fidgeting in the booth. "Can we go now?"

"Our food hasn't even come yet," C.J. replied. "Give it a few minutes. The waitress will be here any second." He hoped.

"I don't wanna wait. I wanna go put up the tree."

Jessica chuckled. "I don't blame her. I was the same way when I was that age. Maybe we should skip breakfast."

"Uh, I already did that. Force of habit." He might as well put on his Failing Parent hat now. "I'm not used to worrying about someone else's meals."

"I understand. I've gotten used to eating for one, too." A melancholy slipped over her features, then disappeared. "Sarah, breakfast should only take a minute and then—" Jessica's cell phone rang and she dug it out of her purse. "Excuse me a second," she said, then flipped it open and answered it.

Sarah crossed her arms over her chest and glared at C.J. "I'm not hungry."

"You need to eat. You're…growing."

"I'll grow tomorrow. Today I wanna put up the tree."

Jessica closed the phone and put it back in her purse. "I've got a little emergency at the store, a mix-up with a delivery. Do you mind if I run over there?"

"Not at all," C.J. said. "In fact, we shouldn't even take up this much of your time, especially during what must be a really busy time of year for you."

"Oh, it wasn't much time." Her gaze traveled to Sarah, and he saw a softening in her features. "Not much at all. Are you sure you'll be okay?"

"All under control." He worked in Hollywood. He could lie with the best of them.

She grinned, clearly not fooled for a second.

"Meet me at the store when you're done and we'll get that tree set up."

"Sure." He caught her eye and they exchanged a smile. A quiet smile, the kind that didn't hold much more than a fleeting connection, but it warmed C.J.'s heart in a way he hadn't thought it could ever be warmed again.

"If I can steal away," Jessica said, "Maybe we can share a piece of pie later."

"That'd be nice." *Nice?* What kind of word was that? Couldn't he have come up with something stronger? More masculine than *nice?*

Way to go, C.J. Definitely win a woman over with power words like nice.

Jessica was gone before he could come up with a sentence redo. And he was left with Sarah, who was watching him with an identical pair of eyes to his own, a pair just as smart and twice as inquisitive.

"You don't know much about kids, do you?" Sarah said.

For a moment he was taken aback by her frankness, then remembered she was Kiki's daughter. Kiki would have raised her to be direct, in-your-face, none of that children-should-be-seen-and-not-heard stuff.

"No," he said, deciding honesty was the best policy, because he was sure this kid could spot a lie at fifty paces. "I don't."

"Then why should I stay with you?"

"Because I'm your dad."

She thought about that for a second. "How do I know that for sure?"

"There's this test with, ah, DNA," he began. Kiki may have said all those years ago that another man had fathered newborn Sarah, but it was abundantly clear the blue-eyed child before him, with the same dimple in her chin and long, thin nose, was his.

"I meant in here," Sarah said, patting at her chest. "Like, how am *I* s'pposed to know you're the right one for me to live with?"

Whoo-boy. She'd asked the one question C.J. didn't have an answer for. He was still searching for that answer in his own life. And hoping like hell he'd find the instincts to be a good dad really, really fast, because he seemed to be lacking those particular characteristics. He wanted to, Lord knew he wanted to, but he wondered whether he even had the ability to be a decent parent. If he could someday finesse a situation—heck, a ponytail—as easily as Jessica did.

"Well, Sarah, that's the kind of thing you sort of figure out after a while. You get to know me, and I get to know you, and we see if we're a good fit and—"

"And what if we're not?" Her blue eyes, sharp on his, the child gone from her voice, as if talking about her future had aged her ten years. But then her lower lip trembled and he realized that she was still very much a scared six-year-old.

And he was still very much a clueless new parent. "Then we'll keep working on it."

"Do I have to move?"

He had known this question was going to come up sooner or later. He'd hoped it would be later, when he'd had more time to prepare Sarah and could find an easy way to break the news of a transcontinental life upheaval. "Yes. I live in California. That's where my job is. And after Christmas, you'll go back there with me."

She shook her head, hard and fast. "I don't wanna."

"You'll like California," he said. "It's sunny all the time. There's a beach not too far from where I live and palm trees and all kinds of things they don't have here in Riverbend."

She toyed with her straw, bopping at the ice cubes in her glass, watching them slip up and down in the water. "I wanna stay with LuAnn."

He sighed. "You can't."

"Why?"

"Because the judge said—"

"I don't care about the stupid judge."

"You have to, Sarah. He makes the rules."

"LuAnn loves me. LuAnn has a room for me. LuAnn makes me pancakes."

"I have a room," C.J. said. "And I know how to make pancakes."

Sarah stared at him, waiting. Then her eyes began to well up, and he knew what he had left off.

That he loved her.

Aw, hell. He barely knew her. He wanted to love her, he really did, but—

But love and C. J. Hamilton had never been a very good fit. He wondered if something was wrong with him. How could a man sit across from his own flesh and blood and not immediately leap to "I love you?"

"I want LuAnn," Sarah repeated, her voice softer, the tears now puddles in her eyes, and C.J. reached across the table for her hand, but she had already withdrawn, pulling into her little six-year-old frame, away from him.

Away from the hurt. He knew that feeling. Knew that look. And especially knew that reflex. His heart constricted, and he vowed to redouble his efforts, to find a way to connect, not just because Sarah needed it—

But because he did, too.

"Sarah—" His cell phone rang, the vibration so startling he jumped back and instinctively reached for the silver Motorola, and the words he should have said got caught in his throat. Too late.

Damn it. When would this get easier?

"Yeah," C.J. barked into the phone.

"Christopher? Don't hang up. Just give me one minute. Please."

C.J. closed his eyes for a second, then drew in a sharp breath, steeling himself for the female voice he had never expected to hear again, especially not given how badly the last conversation had gone, when she'd invited him for some birthday party or something like that, and he'd considered going—until he'd heard the voice in the background that had made it clear C.J.'s attendance wasn't a big priority. "Paula, I—"

"It's Christmas and he's asking for you, really asking for you, Christopher. He needs you."

Across from him, Sarah was ordering pancakes. C.J. held up two fingers, telling the waitress to bring him the same. If only it were that easy to deal with the expectations waiting on the other end of the phone line. C.J. ran a hand through his hair. "He's never needed me before. What makes today any different?"

A state away, in a house large enough for a dozen people that now only held two, Paula Hamilton, John Hamilton's third wife, let out a long, sad sigh. "He's dying. This is your last chance. You can't leave things undone between the two of you."

Dying.

The word slammed into C.J. like a right hook from a welter-weight. John Hamilton had always seemed immortal, living his life hard, at top speed, like the cars he bought, the women he'd chosen before Paula had come along. Apparently all of that fast-track living had finally caught up with him.

But the thought of his father actually dying—

C.J. rocked back against the vinyl of the booth, warring between decades of bitterness and shock, and a wave of impending loss. "My father ignored me for the past twenty years, Paula. Hell, all my life."

"And he'll have to live with that." Ice clinked in a glass as Paula took a drink. For Paula to be indulging before her morning coffee, things did, indeed, have to be very bad. C.J. didn't know the third Mrs. Hamilton that well, but had talked with her a few times and knew she wasn't one to reach for a bottle without provocation. "Will you think about it, please? Make this Christmas special for him. For me. And for you."

"I'm already doing that, Paula. But not with him." Then he hung up the phone and returned his attention to the only relationship in his life that mattered right now—

And given the look on Sarah's face and the way she was ignoring him, one he wasn't doing such a good job of building.

C.J.'s truck let out a groan under the extra weight, but it stopped in front of Jessica's store without losing a single branch. Jessica met them outside, nearly as anxious as Sarah to get the pine inside and set up. As soon as the engine was off, Sarah unbuckled and scrambled out of her seat, then danced her way inside the store, happily holding the door as C.J. carried the bundled pine into the toy shop.

He set it in the tree stand that Mindy had placed in the corner. "We even dug out the ornaments and the tinsel," she had told Jessica with a conspiratorial smile when Jessica returned earlier.

"Wasn't it busy here while I was gone?" She'd glanced around at the crowded shop, the registers making a continual music of sales.

"Extremely. But we managed to find a minute or two to unearth the box of decorations." Mindy grinned. "Now get to decorating."

Jessica rolled her eyes. Mindy couldn't be any less obvious if she was a red flashing light in a snowbank. "Soon as you get back to work."

Mindy had just laughed and returned to the register, humming along with the store's Christmas music as she went.

Within minutes C.J. had the tree perfectly centered and trimmed to exactly the right height to fit the star and still leave a little ceiling clearance. "You act like you've done this before," Jessica said.

"When you work in Hollywood, you work on whatever they tell you. I've done set decorating, costumes, the whole nine yards."

"But you've set up your own tree, too, right?"

He glanced at Sarah, who was mulling over the box of ornaments, taking the decision of which one to hang first very seriously. "I have more than the color of my eyes in common with my daughter." Then he crossed to the box marked Lights and got out the string of multicolored twinklers, instead of elaborating.

She wondered about that, about why he, too, hadn't decorated a tree before, but decided not to ask. Because asking meant getting involved. Connecting. And she wasn't doing that, not with him or anyone, especially not this week.

And yet a part of her wanted to get very involved with C. J. Hamilton. To dream of a future that once again had a man in it, a partner.

A family of her own.

She shook off the feeling. She'd made her choices, and at thirty-seven, it was too late to go back and undo them. Either way, C.J. had made it clear he was going back to California. And that would only leave her alone again because her life was here, in Riverbend.

And right now, her biggest mission was decorating the tree in her store. Not thinking about what-ifs with a man like C.J.

"I can do that," Jessica said, reaching for the lights.

He held them out of her reach, mocking offense.

"What, you think I can't handle this jumble of wires? Who put these back in the box, anyway? A troop of monkeys?"

She laughed. "That would be me, because I'm always in a rush after Christmas to get the tree taken down. The lights get kind of…well, thrown in there."

"You, the woman who takes her holiday so seriously, treats her lights like," he held up the tangled, twisted mess, "this? If I didn't know better, I'd think two cats went to war in this box."

Two of Jessica's regular customers—women who lived just down the street from her—walked by, their arms loaded with toys, and gave Jessica a friendly hello. She returned the greeting, then pivoted back to C.J. "The end of the year is busy for me. Inventory, taxes, closing out the books… And, I have to admit, taking down the lights is not as much as fun as putting them up."

He grinned, then began searching the jumble of green and rainbow bulbs, looking for the plug end. He found it finally and inserted it into the wall, rewarded with a burst of multicolored light along the string. "I believe I have found your one flaw, Jessica Patterson."

"One?" She laughed, but inside, a part of her went warm and soft at the way he said her name. No, not just said it, *caressed* it with his voice. "I have plenty, believe me."

"Can I hang this one?" Sarah inserted herself between them and thrust up a silver angel. "It's so pretty."

"Sure. But after we get the lights on," Jessica replied. "We have to do the lights first, then string the beads, then—"

C.J. put a hand on Jessica's shoulder. "Let her put the ornament up."

"But if she does that first, then we try to hang the lights, the lights get tangled in the ornaments and—"

C.J.'s hand again. "It's just a tree, Jessica, not a science project."

"I have a certain way I like to do…" Her voice trailed off when she noticed Sarah, standing beside the tree, the ornament dangling from her tiny fingers, her pixie face full of disappointment. "I suppose there's more than one way to decorate a tree."

C.J. gave her a smile. One that seemed to take over his entire face, reaching into his blue eyes, lighting them brighter than the lights in his hands. "Definitely more than one."

For a smile like that, she'd have listed a thousand ways.

Whoa.

"Let me, ah, get those lights," Jessica said, taking the string from him, trying more to restring her thoughts back into a semblance of sense.

Customers weaved in and out behind them, shopping the varied displays, looking at the games, the stuffed animals, the connecting block sets, but Jessica barely noticed them. It seemed all that existed was this little world of the three of them—and this tree.

She pulled on the green string, intending to untangle the lights and get busy with the job at hand. Not the man before her. Regardless of where her thoughts might have gone last night, or how many times she had mentally replayed their kiss.

"Wait," C.J. said. "I think I still have—"

"Your—"

"My—"

And somehow they collided, his fingers caught in the jumble of wires, combined with her overzealous untangling, and then they were together, his chest bumping against hers, sending off internal sparks, before they each backed up in a rush. "Sorry," C.J. said.

"My fault," Jessica said, her heart thudding, her pulse thunder in her ears. "Maybe we should, ah, skip the lights altogether."

He grinned. "Or buy all new untangled ones."

Yeah.

Or...keep working on these ones. And try that again.

"Do you like it?" Sarah tugged on Jessica's shirt sleeve. "I made it all pretty. Look!"

A distraction. Well timed and much needed, because Jessica kept getting mixed up in wanting C.J. instead of everything else she was supposed to be focused on.

Like the Christmas tree and staying uninvolved in his holiday—and his life.

The tree. Attention on the tree, Jessica. Not the man standing in front of it.

A three-and-a-half-foot-high perimeter of sparkling ornaments ringed the pine, all placed exactly at Sarah's eye level. It wasn't the perfectly decorated tree Jessica created every year, but it had its own flavor, a child's flavor, and it reminded Jessica of another tree, a long-ago tree, from a Christmas years and years in the past.

Jessica put a hand to her mouth, not wanting the girl to see her caught up in a memory. "Oh, Sarah. It's wonderful. Absolutely beautiful."

And it was, in its own special, unique way. It no longer mattered if the lights had been strung first or the beads were hung. This was, after all, Sarah's first tree, and it was, in her words, boo-ti-ful.

Just as Jessica's first real tree had been.

Christmas music played on the store stereo, creating a soft undertow of holiday spirit, wrapping the tree and all of them in a little magical bubble.

The little girl beamed. "Thank you. Now can we do the star?"

"Absolutely." Jessica dug in the box, came up with the gold topper, handed it to her helper. She hummed a stanza of the song, a burst of Christmas spirit soaring through her heart.

"It's too high. I need a boost," Sarah said, and before Jessica could stop her, the little girl was clambering into Jessica's arms, as easily as a kitten.

Jessica blinked, but took the girl's weight—she had no choice, really—and hoisted her toward the ceiling. C.J. came up behind them, his hand covering his daughter's. The two of them held the delicate star together, reaching as one for the very tip-top. "Let's finish off this tree," he said.

Jessica's gaze met C.J.'s over Sarah's blond curls, and for just a second the magic seemed to leap between the two of them, too. That same enchanted feeling from the night before, with the falling snow, the dark, quiet truck's interior and his kiss—

"Look everyone! See how pretty it is?" Sarah exclaimed.

Jessica pulled her attention away from C.J. "You did it just right, Sarah." She resisted the urge to straighten the slightly askew planetary alignment of the star. It *was* pretty—and exactly the way a six-year-old would hang it.

And that was just fine.

Jessica caught the picture the three of them made, and for a moment she could pretend this was her family—the family that could have been, had she chosen to have children with Dennis. Sarah's blond curls, the color so like Jessica's own. Six years old.

The age Jessica's own child would have been, if fate had had another destiny in mind for the Pattersons. Jessica closed her eyes, inhaled the sweet scent of Sarah's skin and let regret wash over her. For the choices she couldn't undo.

But, oh, if she could go back and choose a different road and have a child like this, a child of her own—

Jessica lowered Sarah to the floor and backed away from C.J. "I, ah, think our tree is all done. How about some hot cocoa?"

"What about the teen-sel?" Sarah asked.

C.J. quirked a brow. "Teen-sel?"

"Yeah, this," Sarah said, digging in the box, and yanking out a container of tinsel so fast and hard the lid opened up, strewing tinsel on the floor, the tree and all over a nearby display of building blocks.

"Oh, no!" Jessica reached for the box, but it was far too late. She'd be vacuuming up this bunch of Christmas spirit for weeks.

Sarah hung her head. "I'm sorry. I just wanted to get the teen-sel on the tree."

"It's okay." Jessica bent and started picking the tinsel off the toys, trying not to grumble about the slippery silver pieces that had wedged between the boxes of blocks. "Really, it's okay." She reassured the girl until Sarah's frown lifted.

"Look at it this way," C.J. said, coming up beside her to help, while Sarah dashed around to get the most wayward pieces. "It's like insta-store decorating."

"Remind me of that when I have to do insta-*un*-store decorating on December twenty-sixth."

"You won't be here to do that, remember?" His gaze caught hers. "Unless you want to stay in town. Then I can help you the day after Christmas, when the shop is closed. We could put on a pot of coffee, order in some pizza, make a day of it."

In his blue eyes, she read temptation. Not just with a little pepperoni and a cup of java, either. "I, ah, have to get this tinsel picked up. It'll wreak havoc with my vacuum cleaner if I don't."

"Aw, you're no fun," C.J. said.

But she wondered how much of that was said in jest, or whether she was just being overly sensitive. Had her funny bone deserted her? Had it gone the way of her Christmas spirit?

What if she did stay in Riverbend this Christmas?

Would she find that funny bone, along with C.J.'s teasing eyes, wrapped and waiting under a tree, much like this one?

Or would both of those gifts be as elusive as the Christmas spirit that seemed to flicker in and out of her heart like a bad electrical connection in a really cheap set of lights?

CHAPTER SIX

IF C. J. HAMILTON had grown up in a house like Jessica Patterson's, he wondered how he would have turned out. Would that wraparound porch, the always-on front light, the welcoming lawn, the big, bright windows, have given him the kind of mental hug he'd never had in real life?

Or if he had a house like this now to come home to, a woman like Jessica waiting for him—

"Are we going in...or just sitting in the driveway?" Jessica asked.

"Sorry." C.J. turned off the engine of his truck and shook off the momentary walk down What-If Avenue. He was supposed to be driving her home at the end of the day, not staring at her house like a loon.

She gave him a curious smile. "You better tell me now."

"Tell you what?"

"What plans you have for my house. I saw the way

you were staring at it. I may not have known you very long, but I already know that means you're up to no good. I've seen every Chevy Chase movie ever created, so I know what you Hollywood types can cook up with a decent lighting and special-effects budget."

He chuckled. "No plans for the house, I promise." He put a finger to his chin. "Though you did give me some ideas."

She swatted him. "Take your ideas elsewhere, Mr. Hamilton."

But the words were a joke, the touch a light one, the mood between them considerably changed from the day before, even an hour before. C.J. glanced down at Sarah, who had fallen asleep between them, her head crooked between the corner of the cushion and the window. "Do you really want to know why I was staring at your house?"

Even though it was early afternoon, and broad daylight, the cramped interior of the truck gave everything between them a hushed feel. She shifted in her seat, her green eyes meeting his, and when they did, his heart skipped a beat. Two. "Yes."

"Because I grew up in a trailer in a not-so-pretty side of Ohio." He glanced again at the Norman Rockwell real estate before him, one more segment of a town that seemed to have been pulled straight out of the very sets he worked on, as if it couldn't possibly be real, even though he was breathing it in, touching it and knowing it was as three-dimensional and real as his own hands. "There was this neighborhood down the street from me, where Mary Klein and Gerry Whitman lived, and all the other kids who had a mom and a dad, and a dog and a cat, and dinner on the table every night." He drew in a breath, surprised at how the memory still stung, like a wound that had never quite healed. "And they lived in houses like these."

She reached out a hand to him, her delicate palm resting on his. How could such a small-framed woman imbue such strength in a simple touch? And how could something so small suddenly move him, nearly to tears, for Pete's sake, over a tiny thing like a house? Four walls, a bunch of windows. Nothing more.

"I'm sorry, C.J. I wish you'd had a house like that."

He turned away. Sucked in a bit of air. "It was nothing. Just a kid, wanting a swing and a dog. All kids do."

"Yeah, they do." Then a shade dropped over her face, and the space between them seemed to stretch to ten feet. "And some kids have that fairy tale and it's not as pretty on the inside as it looks on the outside. And some of them have it and it doesn't last."

He glanced at her, but she already had her hand on the door and was climbing out of the truck. "We better put that tree into some water," she said, "before it starts to dry out. And I'm famished. Let's get some lunch."

Something in what C.J. had said touched on a nerve in Jessica's past. He didn't know what, but it was clear it was a nerve she didn't want to revisit.

He understood that. He had plenty of nerves of his own he'd learned to steer clear of. There were places a man didn't need to go more than once to know he'd been there enough.

C.J. carried Sarah inside and laid her on Jessica's couch, letting her sleep a little bit more. Jessica grabbed the tree stand out of her garage, then they carried the second of the three trees into the house and set it up in her living room, facing a wide bay window that looked out over the street.

C.J. returned from sweeping up the trail of pine needles to find her standing in the center of the room, staring at the tree with an almost wistful expression on her face. "Do you want to decorate it?"

She shook herself. "No. Not now. Let's leave it and have some lunch instead."

C.J. followed Jessica into the kitchen, sure he'd read something in her face a moment earlier but not sure what he'd seen. Maybe there was more to her wanting to skip Christmas than he knew. Maybe he was pushing her too much to do something she truly didn't want to do.

Then his gaze strayed to the sleeping, cherubic child on the sofa, and he thought back to how excited Sarah had been when they'd decorated the first tree, how she'd turned to him after hanging the star, smiling at him, happy for a brief moment—

And knew that no matter what Jessica had going on, he was doing the right thing for his daughter, and right now she had to come first.

"Tuna? Or…tuna?" Jessica asked when he joined her in the sunny yellow kitchen. Bandit trotted over to C.J. for some head-rubbing, plopping down beside him and enjoying all the attention. "I don't have anything in my fridge because I'm leaving tonight."

"About that," C.J. said.

"About what?" Jessica withdrew two cans of tuna, rummaged in a drawer for a can opener, then found a bowl in another cabinet. "You don't like tuna fish?"

"I don't like you leaving."

She sighed, laid the can opener on the counter and turned to him. "C.J., we have been through this a dozen times. It's why I bought the tree with Sarah today, so that you can leave me alone about the whole trip issue. She has that Christmas memory, and it was wonderful, now you can take the reins from here. I'm sure you'll do just fine. But I have my own life to live."

From what he'd seen, she wasn't living much of a life. He'd come in here, intending to talk her into spending time with him and Sarah, because every time the three of them were together, his daughter opened up like a flower, talking more, laughing more.

He knew he should keep the focus on Sarah, but the conversation had taken a detour down a road C.J. couldn't resist, and he found himself treading on personal ground—personal for him and for Jessica.

"What about that life, Jessica?" He took a step closer, invading her space, watching as she inhaled and knowing that he was getting to her. "What kind of life has it been?"

"What do you mean?"

"I've been talking to the people around town, and they say you've become almost a hermit in the two years since your husband died." He took another step closer. Her mouth dropped open in an O of surprise at his words, his invasion of her space, her careful facade. "You run your store, then you go home and stay home. All work and no play makes for a very *boring* life. In fact, no life at all, despite how well you pretend otherwise."

"I don't pretend."

"You don't? It seems to me that you do. You stand here telling me that you're perfectly happy, totally fine, don't mind skipping Christmas at all, yet every time I look in your eyes, I see a woman who feels the exact opposite." He waved toward the door. "Ask anyone in this town and they'll tell you the same thing."

And then she surged toward him, closing the gap, fire in her eyes, crimson sparking her cheeks. "How *dare* you talk about me behind my back like I'm some kind of experiment you want to analyze? How dare you come into my own house and tell me how to run my life?"

"How do I dare? I dare because—" An answering fire had already risen in him, and he stopped trying to tamp it down. He let it come, let it take over him. All day long that fire had been waiting, the embers hot and patient, kept from bursting forth because his daughter had been around, and repeating that kiss in the truck wouldn't exactly be good parenting. But now Sarah was asleep and Jessica Patterson was—

She was *here,* and he was, too, and damn it he was tired of waiting. C.J. took Jessica's arms, bent forward and kissed her, this time not bothering to be soft and gentle, or to couch it in sweet terms, but to tell her, in no uncertain terms, that he wanted her.

His mouth captured hers, hot and hard, nearly a collision of need, instead of the slow introduction of the day before. For half a second Jessica didn't move, didn't respond, didn't seem to even breathe, then the cans of tuna dropped to the tile floor with a hard plop and her hands went around his back and she returned every ounce of what he gave her, twice as intense.

His mind blurred into a swirl of images of her, of her blond hair, her emerald eyes, her lithe, beautiful shape, but most of all, the way the entire package seemed to set off sparks within him.

Sparks of need, never answered by anyone before, as if Jessica had opened a well C.J. hadn't even known existed until she came along.

Sparks of loneliness—because as much as he told her she was pretending to be happy, he knew he'd been doing the same damned thing for way too long.

Until now.

Her tongue dipped into his mouth, playing music against him. A groan escaped his throat, and C.J.'s hands roamed down Jessica's back, along the valleys of her curves, bringing her closer, assuaging for a moment the heat burning inside him. She clutched at his shoulders, holding tight, as if searching for purchase in the storm taking them both.

Eyes closed, he memorized her peppermint taste, her soft, easy lips. He knew, long after this was over, long after *they* were over, that he would come back to this moment and never ever look at the scent or taste of peppermint the same again. God, she tasted good, she felt good—she *was* good.

She was exactly the kind of woman he usually stayed away from because she came wrapped with the bows of entanglement. Permanence. The front porch light, dinner on the table. And as crazy as it sounded, as much as he craved those things, C.J. had always known he wasn't made for that kind of life.

Yet now he had it thrust on him in the form of a child. Was he ready to add to it with a relationship? A relationship with a woman who so clearly came entwined with home, with permanence?

Because to take this any further with Jessica, no matter how sweet the peppermint was, meant doing just that. And if he had no intentions beyond this week, C.J. knew it wouldn't be fair to her to go further than kissing her.

He pulled back reluctantly—because he knew that if he didn't, he'd be going way beyond a kiss a half minute from now—and trailed the back of his hand along the satin skin of her cheek. Oh, how he wished to do more. Much, much more. But he had to be smart, for her sake. Even if he felt as if he'd left his brain cells somewhere back in Des Moines right now.

He traced the outline of her mouth, still tasting peppermint on his tongue. "Apparently, I dare to do a lot more than just *ask* about your life."

A half smile crossed her lips. "Apparently." Then she seemed to recover her wits, returning to some semblance of propriety. She bent down, retrieved the cans of tuna and straightened. "Mayonnaise or relish?"

CHAPTER SEVEN

"MAYONNAISE OR RELISH?" How stupid was that? And what kind of woman asked that question after a man kissed her, for Pete's sake?

Jessica chalked the whole idiotic question up to complete, stunned surprise. She hadn't expected C. J. Hamilton to kiss her. But most of all, she hadn't expected to kiss him back. And especially not like that.

Who was she kidding? She'd been thinking, almost nonstop, about kissing him again, ever since the first time. And now here they were, in her kitchen, doing exactly what she'd imagined—and even better the second time around.

"Mayonnaise," C.J. said.

"Mayo—" Jessica caught herself. "Oh, of course." Her face heated up, so she turned away and busied herself with opening the can, draining the tuna and mixing it with the mayonnaise and some salt and pepper.

All the while replaying that kiss. The riot of emotions and desire that had run through her at C. J. Hamilton's touch. And how very long it had been since she'd felt anything at all like that.

Two years.

C.J. had been right. She *had* been living like a hermit since Dennis died. It hadn't been a conscious decision—just one day after another alone had multiplied atop each other, and it had simply become easier to stay that way, rather than venture into the world of dating again.

Of trying to find another Santa to replace the one she had loved so very much.

"I'm sorry," C.J. said, coming up beside her and sliding two plain white plates onto the counter.

"Sorry for what?"

"For kissing you. That's twice now I've just gone and—" His voice cut off, his gaze met hers, then drifted down to her lips, as if he intended to do that very thing one more time.

Oh, how she wished he would. And at the same time wished he wouldn't.

"I'm a grown woman, C.J. I could have said no."

"But you didn't."

His blue eyes had tiny flecks of silver. Why had she never noticed that before? They looked almost like stardust. No…like snowflakes, tiny snowflakes that fell at the first sign of winter.

"I didn't say no." Jessica moved a step closer to him, the sandwiches forgotten again. "Because you're right. I have been alone a long time. And I've missed having a man in my life."

He quirked a grin. "Any man?"

"Maybe not *any* man."

"Good." He caught a tendril of her hair, wrapped it around a finger, then let it go in one long, slow, silky movement. "You deserve to be happy. Stay for Christmas, Jessica, and let me show you a holiday you'll never forget. One day. What could it hurt, either of us?"

The temptation whispered against her. Stay here, with him. Instead of running away from her memories. From herself, from the fear of being hurt again, left again.

From being left alone in this quiet, empty house.

"I…" The reasons got caught in her throat. In the sparkles in his eyes.

"Just Christmas, Jessica. That's all I ask." He reached down and took her hand, a smile curving across his face. "Look. It's a sign."

Confusion swept over her at the turn in conversation, but then C.J. spun her toward the French doors at the back of her kitchen. They faced her deck, then opened to the dense, wooded lot behind her house.

It had started snowing again. She moved forward, mesmerized, still holding hands with C.J., watching the white flakes drift down from the sky. "I love the first few snowfalls of the season," she whispered. "They're so magical."

He opened the door and they stepped out onto the deck. Big, fat, fluffy snowflakes fell around them, soft and quiet, laying a blanket of white along the ground. It was the kind of snow that fell with a whisper, like hundreds of angelic voices multiplying one on top of the other, nature's own song.

"Look," C.J. murmured again, this time in her ear, his breath warm.

Nearly one with the woods, a doe and her fawn peeked between two trees, then took a tentative step forward, sniffing at the crisp air. The fawn stuck his nose into the new snow, then shook off the fluff, clearly surprised by the wet result of his exploration. He stumbled back, hiding behind his mother's stick-like legs, then peeked again, sneaking stares at the odd humans.

Jessica covered a giggle. "How sweet."

"There's a bit of Christmas magic, right in your backyard," C.J. said, then he turned and smiled, watching her face. "What I see in your eyes right now is what I saw in Sarah's this afternoon. Wonder. Amazement. Joy. If I can just give Sarah that one thing, after all she's been through…" He ran a hand through his hair. "That's all I'm asking of you, Jessica, is to help me. Will you stay, just for Christmas?"

The fawn and doe, probably startled by the human voices, turned, and with a flash of white tails, disappeared into the woods. Jessica went back into the house, rubbing her arms against the chill. Not from the winter air, but from the war inside her. What C.J. wanted was more than Jessica had the power to give.

"Wheat or white?" she asked.

"Surprise me," C.J. said. "As long as you answer my question."

She grabbed a loaf of wheat out of the breadbox and started making a stack of sandwiches. "I can't."

He threw up his hands. "Why? Didn't you have fun today, decorating the tree? Didn't you enjoy that moment outside just now? What is so wrong with spending Christmas here and playing Mrs. Claus one more time?"

She wheeled around. "You really don't get it, do you?"

"Enlighten me."

Then it boiled to the surface, as if the feelings had been waiting there all this time, a teakettle sitting on the back of her heart, just waiting for the right spark to set off that final bubble.

And that spark was C.J.

"Christmas died for me the day my husband did. He *was* Christmas. He wasn't just Santa on Christmas Day, he was Santa all year round. He grew his beard, he wore red, ho-ho-ho'd and he loved those kids." She shook her head, searching for some- thing that would make C.J. understand that for Dennis, Christmas was more than just a day on a calendar. "There's this little boy who lives down the street, Joey Swanson. Four years ago, he was acting up, giving his mother a real hard time. My husband went down there and sat Joey down, just had a con- versation with him and reminded him that it might be August, but Santa was watching."

"What did Joey do?"

Jessica smiled at the memory. She'd been in Hilary Swanson's kitchen that day, sipping coffee, watching Dennis work his magic. "Joey's eyes got wide, because half the kids in this town suspected Dennis was the real deal, you know? Dennis told him that if he wanted to get back on Santa's good list, he needed to do two good deeds to make up for every bad one he'd done. I think he'd broken a window or something like that. But Joey went further than that. He did *three*. Because my husband—*Santa*—had such an impact on these kids."

Jessica paused. "He became Christmas, for me, for the kids, for this town. After he died, I tried to keep up with being Mrs. Claus last year, tried to keep it alive, for his memory, but it was a disaster. I'm not Dennis, I didn't have his touch, his belief that things will always work out. C.J., I can't put on a show and pretend anymore. Christmas just isn't Christmas without Santa."

She turned away, the tears she had held in check for months now falling as fast as the snow outside, dropping onto her counter with plops. They puddled beneath her, blurring her vision. She gave up on lunch and just gripped the countertop, giving in to the grief that held her as surely as she did the laminate.

Grief, not so much for Dennis, because that pain had become more of a dull ache as the months had turned into years, but a grief for the life she used to have. The magic she used to possess. The belief that her life meant something. That she could change things in other people's lives.

Ever since Dennis died, she'd felt like she didn't have the power to change much more than the channel on her television. And given how complicated the surround-sound system was, even that was a challenge some days.

"Oh, Jessica," C.J. said, his arms stealing around her, wrapping her with comfort. Understanding—as if he knew what it was like to lose not just someone, but a part of one's self. "I'm sorry."

She leaned into him, and after a moment her tears stopped, the pain ebbed. "Do you understand now why I can't help you? Why I can't stay in town for Christmas?"

"No, I don't. I think that's all the more reason why you *should* stay. Because what you're looking for, what you feel like you've lost, is still here, Jessica. You just have to find a different way to get it back."

She opened her mouth to argue with him when she spotted Sarah in the entryway. The little girl was rubbing at her eyes, and looking from her father, to Jessica, then back again and not seeming very pleased to see her in the arms of C.J. Quickly, Jessica stepped back and grabbed the plate of sandwiches. "Hey, Sarah! Do you want some tuna fish?"

"No. I don't like it." She frowned. "I wanna go home."

"Sure, sure," C.J. said, seeming just as discomfited by the unexpected arrival of his daughter. He gave Jessica an apologetic smile. "Rain check on the sandwiches?"

"Why don't you just take them with you? I'm leaving and they'll just go bad." She grabbed some plastic wrap out of a drawer, wrapped them up and handed them to C.J. "Late-night snack or something."

"Tomorrow night is the Winterfest," C.J. said. "Seven o'clock, downtown."

"I know. I've lived here all my life."

"C.J., I wanna go home," Sarah said, tugging on his sleeve. "Now." She avoided eye contact with Jessica.

Not a good sign, but how to explain what Sarah had seen? The embrace—even though it had been chaste—between her father and the woman Sarah believed to be Mrs. Claus?

Once again Jessica had disappointed someone, a child no less. Yet another reason not to stay.

"You said you'd give me an opportunity to change your mind," C.J. said to Jessica. "Come downtown, check out the festivities and—"

She shook her head. "My plane leaves at nine."

He grinned. "Then you have plenty of time to stop by and see what I have planned."

Suspicion raised a red flag in her head. "Planned? What do you mean by that?"

He tick-tocked a finger at her. "Now, if I told you, it wouldn't be a surprise, would it?"

"I don't want a surprise, C.J." She didn't want him to convince her to stay. Didn't want to get her heart any more wrapped up in this man and his little girl. Already she was in too deep, and looking into Sarah's eyes, she'd seen what that could cost. How one mistake could hurt, rather than help.

Sometimes, contrary to what you believed, things didn't work out at all. No, they got worse.

But C.J. clearly believed otherwise, because he was still giving Jessica that teasing smile, trying to sway her. "Everyone loves a surprise at Christmas."

Jessica sighed. "I told you, I'm still leaving on that plane."

"And I told you, I wasn't going to let you go

without a fight. Miracles can happen, especially on Christmas." Then he gave her a quick kiss on the cheek, took his sandwiches and his daughter and left.

C.J. stared at Sarah. Sarah stared at C.J. And the third tree, the one that he had bought for Sarah's apartment—which was now his by default—sat in Kiki's living room, unadorned and dropping needles by the second.

Pretty much the metaphor for how things had been going between him and his daughter since the moment he'd arrived in Riverbend.

"I don't wanna decorate it," Sarah said.

"But I thought you had such fun decorating the one at Jessica's store—"

"That's 'cuz she's Mrs. Claus." Sarah crossed her arms over her chest. "And you were kissin' her."

"Uh…yeah, but…" C.J.'s voice trailed off. How was he supposed to answer that? Those parenting books he'd picked up definitely hadn't had a section on what to tell your kid when you were caught kissing Mrs. Claus. Changing the subject was the only tack he knew. "But we still need a Christmas tree at this house, and I bought all these decorations and—"

Sarah plopped onto the threadbare yellow sofa. "It's not the same."

"Sarah, this is our tree. Yours and mine. Don't you want to decorate a tree with your dad?" Even as he said the word *dad,* it sounded weird to his ears. Like a note out of tune.

Apparently, it did to Sarah, too, because she screwed up her face and gave him an odd look. When she called him anything at all, it was still C.J., not Dad. "I don't wanna," she repeated.

He put down the box of ornaments. "How about we go see a movie? Or play a game or—"

"I wanna watch TV." She reached for the remote, flicked on the television and scrolled through the channels until she came to a cartoon. An annoying, nasal-voiced talking sponge appeared on the screen, shouting something about needing to make crabby patties.

"Sarah, I'm trying to talk to you."

She flicked a glance his way, but didn't turn down the volume.

"Do you want to do something?" He was trying here, God help him, but he didn't know quite what to try. "Do something" was a pretty vague statement.

If he'd been a script writer, he'd have been tossed out on his pen for lame use of vocabulary.

The talking sponge went on, now joined by a goofy pink starfish. C.J. didn't see what was entertaining about a sponge in a pair of briefs, but Sarah seemed glued to the television.

He glanced again at the naked tree. The box of ornaments. Out the window at the softly falling snow, the fading sunlight. Christmas would be here before he knew it, and C.J. still hadn't found his miracle. In a couple of days he'd have to head back to L.A. with Sarah. Telling the little girl she was leaving Riverbend, and everything she knew behind hadn't gone well—and why should he have thought it would? He'd hoped that when he had to break that news to her, their relationship would be on firmer ground.

Right now they still seemed to be standing on an earthquake fault.

The only one who had any success in bridging that fault was Jessica Patterson—even if that kiss in the kitchen might have upset Sarah. If he could find a way to bring Jessica back into the picture, just long enough to help him get close to Sarah—and convince his daughter that moving to California would be okay—then maybe that earthquake fault would heal.

If he didn't find a way to stop Jessica from getting on that plane tonight, he'd see the crack between himself and his new daughter widen—

And maybe get too wide to ever close.

Lord knew C.J. needed help in the relationship area. It shouldn't surprise him. His relationship models, particularly parental, had all been as wooden as mannequins and just as cold.

He was working from scratch here and not even sure what ingredients to throw into the mix to make a good father-daughter stew.

No. He did know one starter ingredient. Jessica.

At the same time, his mind whispered how nice it would be to see Jessica again, to have her in his arms one more time. To taste that sweet peppermint mouth. To maybe, just maybe enjoy a little happiness of his own. How long had it been since he had someone in his own life?

He'd confronted Jessica about going home to an empty life—

Because he did the very same thing himself every night.

C.J. pushed the thoughts away. Sarah had to come first. Later there would be time for himself. Yeah, when she was eighteen.

He left the room, picked up his cell phone and put the final touches of his plan in motion. When he finished, he noticed three more messages from Paula. Another earthquake fault, a couple hours away in Ohio.

And another one that would have to wait. Right now he had a ho-ho-hoer to hire, a reindeer to corral and a little girl to wow.

His plan was either incredibly brilliant—or completely insane.

CHAPTER EIGHT

INSANE.

There was only one word to describe Jessica's decision to head downtown when she should be heading to the airport. She'd dropped Bandit at Betty's Bark and Board, then, instead of turning left, she'd turned right, and found herself smack-dab in the center of Riverbend.

It had been a full twenty-four hours since she'd last seen C.J. She'd kept expecting him to turn up, to appear on her doorstep this afternoon, sneaking in among the Concordia Carolers to serenade her with a little "We Three Kings of Orient Are." To stop in for the Last-Minute Door-Buster Toy Sale at her store. To be behind the stack of pepperoni pizzas she'd ordered for her employees for a quick dinner.

But he hadn't. She'd glanced at the tree in the corner of the store a hundred times, missed him twice that much, then chastised herself for even thinking about the man when she should be concentrating on last-minute trip details. But her mind kept going back to his sky-blue eyes instead of ocean-blue waves.

And now, here she was, once again glancing around downtown Riverbend for him, a little stab of disappointment running through her that he had apparently taken her at her word and finally given up. That he was just going to let her go after all.

Jessica parked her car in front of the town hall, buttoned her coat and got out. One more look at Riverbend, she told herself, before she left. A massive wreath hung on the century-old stone building in the center of town, decorated with white lights—one side of which had burned out—and a red bow. She gave the wreath a wry grin, then headed toward the Sit and Sip coffee shop on the corner.

Above her head, miniature versions of the town hall's wreath had been hung on the light poles, connected by garland and huge red velvet bows. Bright-red banners with Happy Holidays written in gold script hung from the poles and swung back and forth in the crisp evening breeze.

Jessica pushed on the door to the shop, expecting the bustling business to be busy and packed, especially on such a cold night. But the store was nearly empty, the tables filled with only a couple of locals.

"Hey, Flo," Jessica said to the owner, striding up to the counter. "Where is everyone?"

"Hi, Jessica!" Flo Brigham's wide smile took over her face, lighting up her brown eyes. The quirky shop owner had tipped her short brown hair with red spikes, probably to celebrate the season, and wore a reindeer-decorated T-shirt and jeans with appliquéd snowmen. Flo, like her coffee shop, never lacked for a bit of festivity. "Most people are already over at the Winterfest. Quite the party there this year, I hear. You planning on going?"

Quite the party? Jessica had never heard the sedate event described that way. She chalked the words up to too much caffeine on Flo's part. "Right now I'm just planning on a cup of coffee. It's getting chilly out there."

"Sure thing. What can I get for you?"

"My favorite of course. A peppermint mocha."

Before Jessica could even get out her wallet, Flo was waving off the money. "On the house. It's the least I can do."

"For what?"

"For you, silly." Flo bustled around the shop's kitchen, pouring the peppermint and chocolate syrups into a cup and then steaming the milk. "You give enough to this town, Jessica. The least I can do is give you a free cup of coffee. In fact, anytime you want a cup, come on by and it's on me."

"I can't let you—"

Flo paused in what she was doing and met Jessica's gaze. "Yes, you can. So don't argue." She slid the mug across the counter. "Enjoy."

Jessica took the cup and slipped onto one of the bar stools. As promised, the peppermint mocha was delicious, a yummy mixture of mint and chocolate, but the suspicions the conversation and the free coffee had raised swirled together in her mind.

And then, two and two made—C. J. Hamilton.

She thought of the tree. Of what Earl Klein had said at the tree lot. Of the mischievous look on C.J.'s face, the way he'd talked about his plan. And now Flo had said nearly the exact same thing as Earl.

"Did C. J. Hamilton come in here by any chance?" Jessica asked.

"Sarah's dad? Oh yes, a couple times. He is just the nicest guy. Knows everybody's name in town, has made about a hundred friends. It's like he's lived here all his life. And he's cute to boot. Why, if I wasn't already a happily married woman, I'd be asking Santa for *him*, that's for sure." Flo grinned.

"And did he say anything?" Jessica took a sip of her coffee, then put the mug down. "About me?"

Flo suddenly got a case of the cleaning bug. She went at her countertops with a vengeance, moving sugar shakers and cream dispensers, scrubbing the surfaces beneath them until they gleamed. "Uh...I can't recall. *Exactly*."

"He did, didn't he?"

"Oh, would you look at the time?" Flo said. "The Winterfest is about to start. I think I'll close up for a few minutes so I can head over and see some of the festivities before the crowds move on down here for a mug or two." She glanced at Jessica. "Aren't you going to set up your Mrs. Claus station?"

Jessica studied the remaining coffee in her mug. "Not this year."

"But the kids will be so disappointed."

"Oh, they'll hardly miss me." She drained the last sips from her drink.

Flo shook her head. "I think you're a bigger part of Christmas than you know, Jessica." She took the empty mug, put it in the sink. "Think about it. Now, do you want to walk over with me?"

"I should..." The wall clock read five till seven. Two hours until her flight. The airport was only twenty minutes away. Technically she did have the time to swing by the Winterfest, maybe say hello to a few friends, before heading out of town.

Uh-huh. That was exactly why she wanted to go over there.

Not because of the curiosity that had built inside her all afternoon, wondering what C. J. Hamilton had up his sleeves.

And why he hadn't at least come by to see her. Where he'd been all day. Moreover, why she'd missed him so much her thoughts had been more on him than Christmas, white sandy beaches—or anything else.

"Sure," Jessica said, sliding off the stool and slipping back into her coat. "Let's go over and see if…uh, see the Winterfest."

Flo shot her a smile that seemed almost conspiratorial, then grabbed her own coat, flipped the sign to Closed and added a little clock saying she'd be back in fifteen minutes, then locked up the coffee shop. The two of them walked down the street and turned the corner that led toward the town park and—

Complete pandemonium.

Riverbend's annual Winterfest was usually fun, but a subdued affair. A few hayrides, an ice-carving contest, hot chocolate served in the bleachers to those listening to the carolers. But what greeted Flo and Jessica this time was the circus version of a Christmas festival.

The entire town had turned out for the event, with people swarming all over the brightly lit, gaily decorated area. The carolers were backed up by the high school marching band, giving a rousing rendition of "Deck the Halls."

A backdrop of dozens and dozens of lighted

displays ran a semicircle around the park. Dancing snowman, arced by a Santa, with his fully loaded sleigh, pulled by the eight reindeer, all in twinkling Technicolor. At each end, bright-green lighted Christmas trees were topped by flashing gold stars. But it didn't stop there.

A full-size lighted train with rolling wheels simulated by flashing bulbs, followed by two boxcars and even a caboose. A jack-in-the-box, springing up at least nine feet off the ground. Another Santa, this one driving a banana-yellow Model-T.

And then there was the live animals. Not just ordinary animals, either. Every single conceivable Christmas-related animal was set up in a mini petting zoo along the right side of the Riverbend Town Park. A camel. Two sheep. A donkey. Jessica half expected the three Magi to come strolling through at any moment.

"Isn't C.J. amazing?" Flo whispered in Jessica's ear. "He did all of this."

"My God," Jessica said. "Are there any lengths this man won't go to?"

Flo grinned. "I don't think so. Like I said, if I wasn't already married—" She grabbed Jessica's arms. "Look! Speak of the devil. Here he comes."

Speak of the devil, indeed. C. J. Hamilton crossed the snow-covered lawn with a confident stride, a tall, imposing figure of a man. He had a way about him, just in his walk, that drew attention, caught Jessica's eye and clearly many other women's. It wasn't simply that C.J. was a handsome man, more that he had a friendly charm, as he greeted several people in the fifteen or so feet that separated them. As Flo had said, he did know most of the townspeople already by name, and he gave each of them a smile and a friendly phrase or two.

C. J. Hamilton wasn't a man who had simply blown into Riverbend like a dandelion seed—no, he'd already planted himself, as surely as the oak that had stood by the town hall for the last hundred years.

Then, when his blue eyes connected with hers, something hitched in Jessica's heart, and she realized the roots C.J. had laid went far beyond the town.

Flo abandoned Jessica, just as C.J. reached them. "You came," he said. The smile on his face read surprise, and joy.

"Looks like the entire town did, too."

"It's kind of hard to miss. I think I might have overdone it."

"Overdone it?" Jessica waved a hand in a wide circle, gaping at the candy apple vendors, dart games, wooden train playground, all lit like downtown Vegas. "This is the kind of display they could see from space."

His grin only widened. "Got your attention, didn't it?" C.J. reached for her hand and gestured to the right, showing her even more that she had missed. Snowmen cutouts where children could pose for photos. A tree-decorating contest. A group of little girls dressed as angels, joining the carolers. "Wait till you see the miniature wooden villages and the reindeer carousel."

"Don't tell me. With real reindeer?"

He chuckled. "Nope. We only have one of those, thank goodness, because Dash is a little hard to handle. This carousel is decked out with fake Comets and Rudolphs."

She spun around, trying to take it all in, the rainbow of Christmas themes nearly a tidal wave of colors and sounds, sweeping over her with one holiday image after another. "How...where... what...? There aren't even words to ask where all this came from."

"I work in Hollywood, remember?" C.J. said. "I'm in the business of pulling off miracles."

"But...this is just..." And then the words did fail her. This wasn't a Winterfest; it was an Olympic Christmas event. "Are those life-size, moving snowmen?"

He nodded. "Animatronics. Wait till you see the gingerbread family behind the bandstand."

"Gingerbread family?" She was starting to feel faint.

"Oh, and the dancing Christmas stockings..."

C.J. chuckled. "A buddy of mine sent those over. Sounded crazy when he suggested it, but it—"

"Stop." She put up her hands. "It's too much. Way too much. You didn't have to—"

"To do what? Throw a huge party for the town? Celebrate Christmas?"

"This is the Vegas version, C.J., Riverbend doesn't need a celebration this big. We're a small town, with small-town expectations."

"Why not? What's wrong with doing it up huge once in a while?" He took her hand again and led her through the center of the park, past the carolers, who had segued into "The Twelve Days of Christmas," complete with a saxophone solo every time they hit the part about the five golden rings. "Look at the kids, Jessica. Look at how much they're loving this. This is every child's dream."

And as she looked around, she saw that the children of the town, were, unquestionably, loving the entire event. They were wide-eyed, darting from thing to thing, petting the animals, heading to ride the fake version, then slipping off as soon as the ride stopped and running to marvel at the lights. There was laughter and impromptu bursts of song, the scent of hot mulled cider and warm chocolate chip cookies.

In the middle of it all there was C.J., watching her response, waiting for her, she knew, to give up her ticket to Miami, to slip into her Mrs. Santa suit and be a part of his winter wonderland.

"What's wrong with huge once in a while?" he asked again.

"You'll be gone after all this is over. When the kids come back next year, expecting the same thing, all they'll get is disappointment."

"If it's about the displays or the cutouts, I can leave those behind and—"

"It's not just about that." She threw up her hands and turned away.

"Then what is it?" When she didn't respond, he touched her shoulder. "Tell me, Jessica."

She drew in a breath, then pivoted, hating that tears had already sprung to her eyes. "My father was a great dad, but he wasn't so good about holding down a job. He had a temper, and when things would go wrong at work, he'd get mad and invariably that would happen just when we'd have a long cold snap or I'd need new school clothes or the rent was due. And all of our security was gone, like that." She snapped her fingers. "You can't just give something *huge* like that and take it away, C.J., kids depend on you. That's the number-one rule of parenting."

"Oh, Jessica." He drew her to him, heedless of the crowds around them. "I'm not trying to do anything more than make magic for the kids."

His shoulder held comfort and warmth, and as

much as she told herself she didn't need either, Jessica sought both in his arms. "What will happen to all of this when you aren't here?" she asked, not meaning who would plug in the lights or who would set up the snowman cutouts.

But what would happen to her. Because she knew, as she held tight to him for one more long second, that Jessica had started to fall for C. J. Hamilton and fall hard.

And that was what scared her the most.

She pulled back. He hadn't answered her question. Because he wouldn't be here next year or even next week, and they both knew it.

"Where's Sarah?" she asked, marveling at how steady her voice sounded even though everything inside her stood on shaky ground.

She couldn't tell by the look on C.J.'s face if he was relieved by the change in subject or not. "Hanging out with Cassidy and Abby Stanley. LuAnn's watching the girls," he said, pointing to the hot chocolate station, where the babysitter was standing with the trio of first-graders. "Sarah's, ah, not talking to me right now. She's still mad at me for kissing Mrs. Claus on the cheek."

"I'm sorry about that."

He shrugged. "I expected a bumpy road. It's just one more bump."

"Do you want me to speak to her?"

"No, I'll handle it. I have to learn to do that anyway, don't I?" He caught her gaze. "It's just hard to explain why Daddy was kissing Mrs. Claus."

A smile curved across Jessica's face at the twist on the familiar Christmas song, then the smile widened at the memory of the kiss, and how wonderful it had been. Geez, here she was, flip-flopping like a mackerel on a boat deck, wanting to run from him one second and run *to* him the next.

Even though they were surrounded by people and lights and a million busy details, the world seemed to close in on just her and C.J., and she wished for a second that he would kiss her again, right now. And refresh her memory. "If I remember right, I was kissing you, too. So that makes me half at fault."

"A mutual mistake?"

"I wouldn't call it a mistake…exactly."

"Good." The smile on C.J.'s face lit a fire in Jessica's gut. Their hands clasped a little firmer, and the distance between them closed a little more.

A thread extended between them, tightening an already taut connection, weaving an intricate pattern of want and complications, wrapping around a sexual attraction that seemed a constant, swirling tempest.

She'd been attracted to Dennis, of course, had enjoyed a healthy sex life with her husband, but hadn't remembered feeling this kind of burning heat every time he looked at her. With Dennis, who had been older than her, their relationship had been one of comfortable shared interests. Dennis had been a tender, compassionate man who had loved her with a quiet easiness.

He hadn't been a man who got in front of her and asked the kinds of questions she never even dared to ask herself. Who lived large—

And dared to ask everyone else to do the same.

"Let me show you something," C.J. said. He led her around the bandstand, past the gazebo, down a familiar stone path that Jessica knew by heart.

"C.J., I told you I didn't want to—"

Before she could finish her sentence, C.J. had covered her eyes. "Stop arguing with me and check out your new digs, Mrs. Claus."

Then he moved his palm. And showed her a miracle.

The little cast-off shed she and Dennis had used for "Santa's Village" had been transformed. Rebuilt, really. It now sported a front porch, a bright-red roof and even green-framed mullioned windows with holly-decorated shutters.

Beside the house was a five-foot-high wire-and-wood-framed pen, holding a reindeer. A real, live, honest-to-goodness, breathing, hoof-stomping reindeer.

"C.J., this is over the top."

As Jessica and C.J. approached, the reindeer threw

up his head, his antlers waving like a spiky halo. "Meet Dash. Your new partner in spreading holiday cheer."

"A real reindeer? Don't you think it's a little much?" But she reached out a hand all the same and gave Dash a pat. The reindeer wanted none of the attention until C.J. showed her a bag of carrots by the side of the pen and helped her feed one to the hungry animal. "Now, one more thing to see. Inside."

She shook her head, knowing what he had planned next. She had a plane ticket in her purse. Plans that were too late to change. Already she was too involved, too wrapped up with him. Too tempted. "I can't—"

"Yes, you can." He led her forward, up the new brick path, pressing on the brass handle and opening the red door to reveal a bright, freshly painted golden room that held a pair of high-backed claw-footed velvet chairs.

The original chairs. The same ones she and Dennis had sat in for fifteen years, refurbished and buffed to look like new. A sharp pang hit her chest at C.J.'s thoughtfulness and care. The way he'd worked to create the perfect Santa environment because he'd known how important it was to her. Still, her Christmas spirit had deserted her and—

Then she noticed the last detail.

The suit. He'd gone and found her suit.

The familiar red crushed-velvet outfit, framed with faux white fur hung on a padded satin hanger against the wall. Above it, her Mrs. Claus lace-trimmed cap dangled from a hook, while her black lace-up boots waited on the floor below. C.J. had thought of, quite literally, everything. She looked at him, on the verge of tears, moved beyond words. "Oh, C.J. How did you…?"

"Mindy helped with that," C.J. explained. "She knows where you keep your extra key and also where you store your suit in the off season. She had it dry-cleaned and everything. All it needs now is the Mrs. Claus to fill it."

She opened her mouth to argue, but he put up a finger and stopped her.

"No one else fits it like you do, Jessica. No one else can be Mrs. Claus but you." He took her hand and led her to the window, then pulled back one of the holly-and-ivy-patterned curtains. "Tell me what you see."

"Decorations. A carousel. Snow."

"No. Children. A whole lot of children who are waiting for Mrs. Claus. For *you*."

She backed away, drawing her hand out of his grasp. "Believe me, I was never the main attraction. It was always Santa. And without a Santa—"

"I thought of that, too." C.J. released her to grab a big white box from the corner. He pulled off the cover, revealing a shiny new Santa suit, wig and beard. "You said you needed a Santa and here's one right here."

She gaped at him. "You'd go that far? To play Santa? Just to give Sarah a good Christmas?"

"Oh, no, not me. Earl Klein volunteered for the position. I'm strictly a behind-the-scenes kind of guy."

The expression on his face told the story—C. J. Hamilton had built the set, written the script, provided the costumes and even hired the actors. Now he expected Jessica to step into the role and carry out the story he envisioned.

A story that was still lacking one critical element. If it was going to work, it had to be right.

"Santa's Village is due to open in five minutes," C.J. said. "Earl should be here any second. So if you could just slip into—"

She crossed her arms over her chest. "No. I will not let Earl Klein be Santa. He's a nice man, but he's not Santa material."

"Why not? I met the man. He's affable, friendly—"

"And he can't remember the names of the reindeer, has no gift for storytelling, and wouldn't be able to point out a single child in this town if you paid him. It takes more than niceness to play Santa. It takes a special quality to be the big guy. You can't just throw on a red suit and a white beard, let out a couple of ho-ho-hos and be believable."

"How hard is it to remember Rudolph, Dasher, Dancer, Prancer, Vixen, Donder, Blitzen, Cupid and

Comet?" C.J. said. "And to whip up a little fiction about an elf who got a little overzealous with the marshmallow, and that's why all the teddy bears this year are white?"

"It's not that…" Jessica's voice trailed off. She stared at C.J., seeing the man with new eyes. "Tell me your favorite Christmas memory."

"Jessica, we don't have time for this." He glanced out the window. "In fact, there's Earl coming right now. The kids will be here any minute. You need to—"

"Tell me one memory. Just one."

An exasperated sigh whooshed out of him. "I can't."

"It's not that hard, C.J. Just one."

"I can't tell you my favorite Christmas memory because I don't have one."

"Oh, everyone has a favorite." She trailed a hand over the box holding the Santa suit, knowing she was crazy for even considering what she was thinking, for staying here one second longer. "I don't need to hear about every Christmas between when you were three and thirteen. Pick one."

"I'm not kidding, Jessica." He glanced again out the window, then grabbed her suit off the hook and pressed it into her hands. "Can you just get ready?"

"Not until you tell me." Why was she delaying?

Why wasn't she running to her car? She was going to miss her flight at this rate.

Yet curiosity burned inside her, a gnawing to know more. To know what C. J. Hamilton was keeping hidden.

His gaze went to the window, then back at her, frustration clear on his features, but she waited, knowing with some instinct deep inside her that C. J. Hamilton held memories he'd never shared, or maybe had shared with very few people. And that sharing them with her would make all the difference—

In helping to build that bridge with Sarah.

She knew, because once upon a time, someone had done that with her.

"I've never had a Christmas, all right?" C.J. said finally, his voice gruff as sandpaper. "I can't remember a tree, anyone telling me Santa was on his way down the chimney. No waking up at the crack of dawn, to tear open a stack of gifts. For years I'd get up just in case, because, like an idiot, I believed, like lots of kids do, that Santa would come anyway, but there was never anything. After a while I got smart and I gave up looking."

Shock stunned her into silence. She'd expected a dozen different answers—none of them the one she'd heard.

"Oh, C.J.," Jessica said, dropping the Mrs. Claus

suit onto her chair and going to him, her heart hurting for him. "Didn't your grandparents or your parents—"

"My mother died when I was a baby. My father had…other priorities, and that destroyed any other family relationships he might have had." C.J. sank into one of the velvet chairs, his shoulders hunched forward. "After my mother died, my father went right back into the bachelor life, running around, staying out all night, forgetting he had a kid to raise. So I pretty much raised myself, because he was never there.

"I understood what you said about living a life of insecurity because mine was a lot like that too. Only, not because my father didn't keep a job—but because he blew his paychecks on liquor and women. When I was in college, he hit the lottery. Made him a rich man overnight. He tried to give me money, maybe out of guilt, but I wouldn't take a dime. He got married for a second time, got divorced, then met Paula, who straightened him out, I think."

She knelt beside the chair. "You think?"

"I haven't spoken to my father in almost twenty years. At least not face-to-face."

Jessica gasped. "Why?"

He met her gaze. "When I say I never had a Christmas, Jessica, I mean I *never* had a Christmas. No trees, no presents, nothing. My father either didn't have the money or he forgot. By the time he got a clue, I was an adult and it was too late." C.J. shook off the bitterness in his voice. "I tell myself it doesn't matter. And when every December rolls around, I just pretend the holiday doesn't exist. Living in California, it's a little easier to do. When I was with Kiki, she was as unconventional as they came, and back then she had this whole thing against the commercialism of Christmas, so we didn't celebrate the holiday."

"You have *never* celebrated Christmas?" The thought was too unbelievable to grasp.

"I've never had a reason to." Then his gaze strayed out the window and back toward the Winterfest, back to where Sarah was sipping hot chocolate and laughing. "Until now."

So much of Jessica's life had revolved around Christmas. Dennis had made it his entire year, really. She spent days in a store dedicated to the holiday. And here was a man who hadn't had so much as a tree, hardly a present. "All of this was about more than just getting me to stay, wasn't it? It was for you, too."

He shook his head. "No, I don't need it. It's all for Sarah."

A muscle twitched in C.J.'s jaw, the only fissure in his steel composure. Somehow, that broke Jessica's heart more than if he had sat down and sobbed. She could see the stoic little boy he must have been, the chin-up child who'd gone on ever December twenty-fifth as if he didn't care that his father—and Santa—had forgotten him. Again and again.

C.J. rose and pulled her up with him, his blue eyes meeting hers. "That's why I want Sarah to have the best Christmas ever. I refuse to let her grow up like I did. It's not just about being a good dad. Or starting our relationship off on the right foot. It's about her having the life all little girls deserve."

And little boys.

Jessica looked at the Mrs. Claus outfit draped over the chair. Thought of the plane tickets in her purse. Plane tickets that no longer mattered, not nearly as much as the man in front of her. She'd make a call, take a later flight and stay here long enough to provide one more key to the perfect Riverbend Winterfest.

Not just for the children of the town, or for Sarah, but for C.J. In his eyes, she saw the young boy C. J. Hamilton had once been. A boy who had woken up a dozen years in a row, with hope undoubtedly hanging stubbornly in his heart as he crept down the stairs, wondering if maybe, just maybe, Santa Claus might have found him after all.

And that there might have been one miracle by his chimney. One gift. One little stocking stuffer. And finding only the same empty living room as the day before, the year before.

Not this year, she vowed.

"You deserve it, too," Jessica said softly, her hand stealing into C.J.'s. "You deserve that life, too, C.J."

Tears filled his eyes, but he swallowed, and the moment of weakness disappeared. "Jessica, I—"

"I'll stay and be Mrs. Claus," she went on, cutting off his objection. "But on one condition."

His lips curved upward. The rainbow of Christmas lights played across his features. "What's that?"

"You fire Earl." She leaned forward, cupped his jaw, then placed a quick kiss on his lips. "There's only one man I know who has enough magic in his heart to play Santa this year."

CHAPTER NINE

No one had told him the beard, the wig and the fuzzy eyebrows would itch like a bucket of fleas on his head.

But then again, C.J. would never have expected that he'd be the one playing Santa, either. Yet here he was, sitting in the opposite armchair to Jessica's, while children climbed into his lap, ho-ho-hoing and giving a jolly good impression of the big guy, if he said so himself.

For someone who'd never so much as waved at a mall Santa, C.J. had to admit he wasn't half-bad at the job. Jessica helped him out by filling in when he blanked on a fact, or stumbled over a name, but more than that, helped him through the whole process with her calming presence. Simply having her beside him made the entire process easier.

Hell, having her anywhere near him made walking on the moon seem possible right now. In between children, he caught her eye, and found himself thinking about things that had nothing to do with Santa or Christmas but a whole lot to do with wishes. For time alone and a way to thank her for giving him a gift he couldn't quantify.

"And I want a pony and a monkey and a new bike and a dollhouse and a baby bear and—"

"Whoa, whoa," C.J. said, interrupting the little girl before him—and bringing his thoughts back to being Santa, not Jessica. "That's a pretty long list for Santa. I can't fit all that in the sleigh."

The girl considered. "Okay. Then I want just the pony and the monkey."

"Uh…" C.J. glanced at the girl's parents, who had that panic-stricken, no-way-we're-installing-a-barn-in-the-backyard look on their faces. "My elves don't make live animals in the workshop. But if you can think of a toy you'd really like—"

The girl shook her head so hard, her brunette curls bounced like pogo sticks. "I wanna pony."

"Real live ponies are a lot of responsibility," C.J. said, scrambling for a win-win solution. "What if Santa brings you a toy pony—" he glanced at the girl's parents for a nod of affirmation "—and you show me how well you can care for that, and then we can talk again next year about the real thing."

The girl's eyes became as big as saucers. "You promise?"

"Well, we'll have to see about that." C.J. leaned down. "Can I let you in on a secret?"

She nodded. "Uh-huh."

"The reindeer get pretty jealous if I pay attention to other animals. That's why I have to stick to toys only."

"Oh," she said, drawing the word out in one long syllable. "That's why there's no kittens or puppies in the sleigh."

"Exactly. So you can imagine the problems a pony might bring."

The girl thought about that. "Okay. A toy pony. And will you talk to Dasher and Comet and Rudolph so someday I can get a real pony?"

C.J. chuckled. "I will. If you promise to take real good care of that toy pony and show me you can be super-duper responsible."

She beamed. "I will. I promise. Merry Christmas, Santa!" She pressed a quick kiss to his cheek, took a candy cane from Jessica, then hurried off his lap and over to her parents, talking a mile a minute about the reindeer and ponies, and why never the twain should meet.

"You handled that really well," Jessica said. "I'd never have thought of that reason."

"When you work in Hollywood, you have to be inventive." He loved the way her eyes twinkled when she smiled, the red in her cheeks, the soft undertow of laughter in every one of her words. Playing the jolly St. Nick's wife clearly agreed with her.

And, C.J. had to admit, with him. He'd never had much involvement with Christmas, that was true, but he found himself enjoying the charade, getting wrapped up in the tales he told the children, the role he played. Christmas spirit practically flowed through his veins.

He glanced over at Jessica, grasped her gloved hand with his own and caught her gaze. "In case I forget to say it later," he said, "thank you."

The smile that took over her face was worth a thousand Christmases. "You're welcome."

Before he could say anything more, or tell her how the last few hours had changed something fundamental in him, exposed a side of his self that he hadn't even known existed—

The door opened and LuAnn entered, Cassidy and Sarah by her side, with Abby bringing up the rear. C.J. hesitated. He hadn't planned for his own daughter to make a Santa visit. But of course she would, given how much she had talked about it in the past couple of days, according to LuAnn. Oh boy, what if she guessed it was him beneath the white beard?

Cassidy, the bolder of the girls, hurried over to him first, clambering onto his lap, demanding a slew of Barbie dolls before climbing down just as quickly and accepting a candy cane from Jessica. "I've been very good," Cassidy pronounced. "I didn't even eat the last piece of my birthday cake. Yet." Then she was gone, back with LuAnn, her Christmas morning clearly assured. Abby changed her mind at the last minute, still a bit afraid of the whole Santa experience.

Sarah headed over, exchanging a secret smile of identity knowledge with Jessica before she approached C.J. He froze, sure his daughter would recognize him.

"Hi, Santa," she said, her voice quiet and soft, shy.

"Hello, Sarah." C.J. forced a little deepness into his voice, a ho-ho-ho tone to the ending notes. "Would you like a seat?" He opened his arms and invited her up.

She nodded, then climbed into his lap. "I missed you last year."

"Had a bad case of the flu. I was really sorry not to be here, but I had to get well so I could be out delivering toys on Christmas Eve."

Jessica gave him a smile, clearly glad for the save that explained the missing Santa.

"Tell me what you want for Christmas," C.J. said, relieved that his daughter hadn't seen past the disguise.

He expected her to name a toy, another stuffed animal or a unicorn to add to her collection. Or a few Barbie dolls to help her rival Cassidy's collection.

But Sarah didn't leap to a long list of toys. Instead she paused to think, her blue eyes wide with earnestness. "I want everything to be the same."

C.J.'s mouth went dry. No ready reply came to mind. "Everything to be the same? What do you mean by that?"

"I know my mommy's in Heaven," Sarah said, and the sadness in her voice nearly made C.J.'s heart break in two, "and she can't come back, but—" she lowered her voice, nearly to a whisper "—I don't want my new dad."

Now his heart really did break. It tore, right down the center, ripping through his gut, shattering like crystal. He had to hitch a breath, hard, just so he could talk. Beside him, he heard Jessica let out a little gasp. "And, ah, why is that?"

"'Cuz he wants to move to Cali...Cali..." She stumbled over the four syllables of the unwieldy state name.

"California," he supplied, hating the word even as it slipped past his own lips. Wishing it wasn't so far away. That he had the power to pick up the state, move it next door.

Anything to wipe away that look in his daughter's eyes. Erase the disappointment. Hurt.

Sarah nodded, as somber as a judge. "And I don't wanna. I wanna stay here. I wanna live with LuAnn. Will you talk to him, Santa? And tell him I wanna stay with my friends and my unicorns and my bed and my toys and my room?"

He swallowed, but his mouth had gone dry. What a fool he had been, thinking that he had been doing such a good job, working to build Sarah's trust, connecting with her—

Becoming a father. As if it was as simple as turning on a switch.

When the truth was that he had failed as badly as his own father had.

"Sarah, I—" But the words weren't there. What could he say? Yes, he'd restore her life as it had been? Sign over custody to the babysitter who stood by the door, her eyes welling in sympathy?

Or, no, he wouldn't give Sarah that gift, instead he'd force her to go with the father she didn't love, make her move to California and leave behind everything she knew? "Oh, Sarah—"

"Santa will make sure you're happy on Christmas morning," Jessica said, laying a comforting hand on C.J.'s arm. "Because that's what Santa does."

"Does that mean I get to stay here?" Sarah asked, hope arching over every word.

"Only Santa knows that answer. But I'm sure he'll talk to your dad and everything will work out exactly as it's meant to be." Jessica gave Sarah a comforting smile, then pressed a candy cane into her hand. "You have a big job ahead of you, though."

"I do?"

Jessica nodded. "You have to work extra hard to get to know your dad. Because Santa tells me he's a very nice dad and he loves you very, very much. And he wouldn't do anything that would make you unhappy."

"But he wants to move to me to Californee-ya."

Jessica leaned forward and cupped a white-gloved hand around Sarah's jaw, then met C.J.'s gaze for a second. "Talk to him, Sarah. Tell him how you feel, and I'm sure you can work it out. Besides, I hear California is a lot of fun. Santa even likes to vacation there from time to time. He's quite the surfer." Jessica winked, and Sarah giggled at the thought. "Okay?"

"Okay. Thank you, Mrs. Claus. Thank you, Santa," Sarah said. "And Merry Christmas." Then she gave C.J. a quick kiss on the cheek and hopped off his lap.

C.J. watched his daughter go, his heart as shredded as the hay in Dash's stall. He should have been overjoyed—Sarah had, after all, just given him her first burst of affection.

Too bad it had been delivered to his alter ego, and given with the wish that she get anything other than him for a Christmas gift.

An hour later, C.J. and Jessica closed up Santa's Village and changed out of their costumes. He'd had more fun than he could have even imagined. Heck, next he'd be masquerading as the Easter Bunny.

C.J. caught up to Jessica as she was crossing the town square toward her car. "Thanks for playing Santa," Jessica said. "Now I really do have to catch my flight. There's a beach waiting for me."

"Why did you say that?"

"Say what?"

"That I would reconsider moving Sarah to California."

"I didn't say that exactly."

"You implied it with that whole 'Santa will talk to your dad' thing. I don't want Sarah thinking that I'm going to stay in Riverbend. My job is on the West Coast. She has to move."

"And you have to be a parent. That means reorganizing your priorities."

"What the hell do you think I'm doing here?" He threw up his hands in frustration. It seemed no matter how many steps he took forward, he ended up taking five steps back. And now Jessica had gone and added a quagmire to the mess he already had with Sarah. "Besides, who are you to tell me how to be a parent? You aren't one."

She recoiled as if he had slapped her, and immediately C.J. wanted to take the words back. "I'm sorry, Jessica. I shouldn't have said that."

"No, you're right. I'm not a parent and I have no right to tell you how to be one. I should mind my own business and stay out of yours."

They were alone. The Winterfest had ended around the same time Santa's Village had closed up, and most of the town had gone home, leaving only a few people wandering the park, looking at the lights. But here, in front of the town hall, the streets were empty, Riverbend locked up tight for the night. The snow had stopped falling and all was silent and still, as quiet as a church. C.J. took a step toward Jessica. Her hair was a little askew and flyaway from wearing her Mrs. Claus cap and wig, making her look wild and sexy all at once.

"I don't want you to do that," he said, the anger gone as quickly as it had appeared. Whatever problems he had with Sarah were not Jessica's fault, after all.

"To do what?"

"To stay out of my business. I don't want you to stay away, period."

She shook her head, and the easy camaraderie of earlier disappeared from her face. Already she was inserting distance between them, building an intangible wall. "It's best if I do."

"Why?" He took another step closer, capturing her hands, warming her chilled fingers with his own. He didn't know where her gloves were—probably forgotten back in the shed—but he was damned glad she didn't have them on now because he wanted to touch her, feel her against him, any way he could.

"I shouldn't get involved with anyone right now."

Neither should he, his better sense whispered, but he ignored it. Because her hands were in his, and he'd stopped thinking straight about the time she touched his cheek and told him he, too, deserved a real Christmas.

Something had shifted in C.J. today, something monumental that he hadn't time to examine yet but knew whatever it was meant a change, a fork in the road he'd always followed.

"How long are you going to protect your heart, Jessica?"

"I'm not—"

"You are. Your husband has been gone for two years, and yet you're still alone. I know, because I've done the same thing all my life, and I didn't even realize it until that lawyer showed up on my doorstep and told me I had a daughter. Then all of a sudden, I had a relationship, someone who needed me to figure out how to connect. Then I met you. And you added—" he grinned "—a whole other complication. But every time I get close, you back away. Or remind me that you're leaving."

"Why should I bother? You're just going to leave, aren't you? Go back to California. That's not exactly around the block, you know."

"It's my job. I'm not abandoning anyone."

"That isn't how it feels." She turned away, pulled out of his grasp and started toward her car again.

C.J. sighed. He couldn't win. How could he make Jessica see that he had begun to care—about her, about Sarah—and that just because he had to return to California, it didn't lessen those feelings?

As she walked away, another thought struck him, so hard it could have been a giant lightbulb in a cartoon. "Why do you do it?"

She pivoted back. "Why do I do what?"

"Surround yourself with children, when you don't have any of your own? Is it because—" he hesitated "—because you can't have children?"

She didn't say anything for a long, long time. Then she let out a breath, frosted with the chilled air. "It wasn't me."

He waited, silent, for her to go on.

"Dennis was impotent. He was in an accident when he was a teenager and it turned out he was never able to have kids. We didn't find out until we started trying, after we'd been married for a while."

"But there are other options. In vitro, adoption."

"I knew that and Dennis was willing to do anything, but I said no. To be honest, I was relieved." She turned away from C.J. and went to the bench by the hot chocolate station, sinking onto the wooden seat. "What kind of woman says that? Relieved that her husband couldn't father a child?"

"A woman who had her reasons, I'm sure," C.J. replied, seating himself beside her.

"Fear," she said, so softly he almost didn't hear her. "Fear that I'd end up like my mother, trying to feed a child with nothing. Heat a house with sticks. Make a Christmas out of paper dolls and other people's charity."

"But you're successful, you're fine."

She spun on the seat. "I'm not. Look what happened, C.J. My husband died and left me—alone. And Dennis, who did such a good job caring for everyone else in the world, did a lousy job caring for himself. He hated going to the doctor, ignored the warning signs, heck, the warning *billboards* his heart kept sending him, and didn't leave so much as a dime of life insurance. I had a business to run, employees to worry about. If I'd had a child to care for, too—" She shook her head.

"You'd have made it work," he said, laying a hand on hers.

"How do you know that for sure? My mother tried, and she failed. We ended up collecting welfare and even that wasn't enough sometimes." She rose, drawing her coat tighter around her, shutting him out as she did. "I can't get involved with you, or anyone else. I can't take a chance like that and end up—" she blew out a breath, her eyes misty "—alone again."

"But you already are alone, Jessica."

"At least it's an alone I know. There aren't any

surprises this way." She turned on her heel and began heading toward her car again.

"Now who's running out on who?" he said to her retreating figure, frustrated that this woman, who drove him crazy and who needed—and deserved— love in her life more than anyone he knew, pushed it away like it was a hot stove waiting to burn her.

She turned back. "You said I'm the one who needs to open up my heart, C.J., but I think you still have a few wounds to heal of your own before you start telling me about mine." Her gaze softened. "It's Christmas. Maybe you should call your father and tell him he has a grandchild. Give him a chance to start over again with a second generation."

"I doubt that would make much of a difference. He's not a man who changes easily."

Her gaze narrowed. "Why have you never had a Christmas?"

"I told you about my father, my childhood."

"No, I meant after you grew up. You could have gone to a Christmas party. Bought your own tree, heck, built your own winter wonderland in your backyard, but you never have. Why?"

He scowled. "What is this, twenty questions?"

"Oh, you can probe into me, but vice versa doesn't apply?"

She was right—and he hated that she was right. He'd asked her plenty of tough questions just a second ago, and Jessica had been honest. All she wanted in return was the same.

He gave her a lopsided grin. "I guess we're more alike than different, Jessica. I didn't want to be disappointed. To find out it didn't measure up to all I'd imagined."

"Oh, C.J., it's all that and more," she said, a soft, sweet smile on her face. "Believe in yourself, in what you can do, as a father. After all, wasn't it Santa—or a man pretending to be Santa—who told me just the other day that miracles can happen, especially on Christmas?"

He chuckled. "Using my own words against me?"

"Whatever works." Jessica smiled, then sobered. "I hope you work things out with Sarah. She's a wonderful girl, an unbelievable blessing." Jessica put a warm hand against his cheek, then replaced it with a kiss of goodbye.

CHAPTER TEN

"O LITTLE TOWN OF BETHLEHEM" played on the loudspeakers, an odd juxtaposition to the laughing swimmers in the pool, the hot sun beating down on Jessica's body and the waiters weaving in and out of the dozens of lounge chairs with trays of umbrella-decorated drinks.

December twenty-third, two days before Christmas, and Jessica was down in Miami, as she'd planned; yet, even here, she was as surrounded by the holiday as she had been back home.

Except here the wreaths dangled from the palm trees and the snow was made of sand. The snowmen were plastic, the Santas sweated in their costumes, and the twinkling lights competed with the evening neon signs.

She should have been happy. Laughing, smiling, like the dozens of people surrounding her at the luxury resort. But she was miserable.

Depressed even.

She missed the streets of Riverbend. Missed the children. Missed the decorations. And yes, God help her, she even missed the snow.

And most of all she missed Sarah and C. J. Hamilton.

"Ma'am? Is there anything I can get you?" The waiter stood before her, blocking the bright sun, providing a moment of shade. Of respite, sanity.

"Yes," Jessica said, feeling like she could finally think straight. "There is. A telephone."

The truck bumped over the rough road, as if it didn't want to make the journey any more than C.J. did. Sarah had fallen asleep about five miles earlier, her blond head using C.J.'s right arm as a pillow. At a stop sign, C.J. glanced down at Sarah and realized that at some point having Sarah in his life had become a constant, no longer a surprise.

When had that happened? When had he gone from C.J., single man, to C.J. and Sarah, package deal? About the same time, he realized, as he took in her cherubic features and felt everything within him melt like a spring thaw, when he had started to love his daughter.

And he knew exactly when that had happened, too. When she had broken his heart back in that little shed at Santa's Village.

How ironic. And yet how true. Wasn't there a saying about knowing you loved someone the minute they were capable of shattering that very same heart?

He reached out his arm and drew Sarah as close as the seat belt allowed. Tucking her against his side, he bent down to inhale the Johnson & Johnson scent of her golden curls. Somehow, he vowed, he'd find a way to make her happy. A perfect compromise for all of them.

Just as Santa had promised.

A beep sounded behind him and he drove on, coming far too quickly upon the turn he sought. He stopped the truck in front of the palatial two-story house in the woods, its glass front looking out over the beautiful Ohio landscape. Money dripped from every balustrade and perfectly landscaped shrub, a testament to the power of the dollar to buy beauty.

But not happiness.

C.J. roused Sarah, who rubbed at her eyes and stared at the unfamiliar surroundings. "Where are we?"

"Your grandfather's house."

"Kiki's daddy? Isn't he in heaven, too?"

Kiki's parents had died when she was a teenager, her father of a drug overdose, her mother following in his footsteps a few years later, a real-life Romeo-and-Juliet ending. Kiki had grown up in a turbulent home and ended up living a turbulent life of her own.

Frankly, C.J. was surprised Sarah had turned out as well adjusted as she was. Clearly, Kiki had done her best when it came to her own child. "No, not Kiki's daddy. This is my father's house," C.J. explained.

"Where's your mommy?"

"She died when I was a baby."

Sarah turned to him. "So you're like me, and you don't have a mommy, either."

The words hit him harder than he expected, and C.J. swallowed, then bent to catch his daughter's gaze, realizing a connection that went beyond their DNA. "Yeah, Sarah, just like you."

She reached out then, wrapping her arms around his neck and hugging him tight. Tears stung at C.J.'s eyes. Holy cow. Sarah was hugging him.

No. *His daughter* was hugging him.

Such a simple gesture of sympathy, and yet it moved him more powerfully than a tidal wave. He held her tiny frame tight, giving back the same warmth. Two motherless children, decades apart, yet each needing the other. More than they probably knew.

After a moment Sarah drew back, then glanced out the window, picking up her stuffed unicorn off the seat and clutching it tight to her chest. "Do you think he'll like me?"

"Of course he will. Because I do. In fact…" He caught one of her curls around his finger, then cupped her jaw. "I love you, Sarah."

Sarah stared at him.

C.J. told himself it didn't matter if she ever said the words back. That he didn't care, because *he* loved *her,* and he'd finally found the words to tell her.

But then Sarah surged forward with a second hug, this one so tight it nearly took his breath away. C.J's heart swelled, then almost burst when Sarah whispered in his ear, "I love you, too, Daddy."

And C.J. realized it did matter. A lot.

C.J. held tight to that hug, those words, for as long as he could. Someday, he knew, she'd grow up and be gone. But he'd never forget this moment.

Everything else in his life paled in comparison. There was no award he could win. No prize he could be handed. No dollar amount he could imagine that could ever be as magnificent as the gift of Sarah.

Before releasing her, C.J. glanced out the window. And mouthed a heartfelt thank-you heavenward.

"Come on, kiddo." C.J. cleared his throat, ruffled Sarah's hair. "It's time to go in." He got out of the truck and came around to the other side to help her down. Then C.J. took his daughter's hand and together they climbed the granite steps to ring the doorbell. A symphony pealed inside, announcing their arrival.

Paula opened the door immediately, as if she'd been watching for them. "C.J.! You came."

"I brought along someone else, too." He gestured

to Sarah. "This is Sarah, my daughter. Sarah, this is Paula, your…" He glanced at his third stepmother, not sure what designation, if any, she wanted.

"Grandma is fine. If it's okay with you." Paula's smile wobbled a little on her face, as if she were unsure whether she would be included in the family, and C.J. decided it was time he stopped judging Paula from a distance and widen the circle.

"Grandma," C.J. agreed.

Sarah beamed. "I like having a grandma. I never had one before."

"And I like having a granddaughter." Paula returned Sarah's smile, with a stronger, firmer version this time. C.J. met Paula's gaze and gave her a nod of thanks and friendship. Her eyes welled up briefly, but then she whisked the tears away before bending down to Sarah's level. "Can I get you something to eat, Sarah?"

"Do you have peanut butter? And jelly?"

"Peanut butter and jelly? Why those are my favorites. I'm sure we do." She put out her hand. "Let's head into the kitchen and let your dad visit for a little while by himself. Okay?"

C.J. watched the two of them head down the hall, Sarah wide-eyed and clutching her unicorn. When they were gone, the house fell silent, save for the regular clicking of a machine coming from a room to his right. C.J. drew in a breath, then followed the sound, feeling the gap of years close with every step. "Dad?"

When C.J. rounded the corner, he came to a sudden halt, breath lodged in his throat. A stranger lay in the bed, slashes of sunlight from the blinds seeming to carve him into pieces. John Hamilton had become skinny and pale, dwarfed by sheets and pillows. The last time he had seen his father, John had been tall and strapping, his booming voice still carrying the same authority as his presence. But illness and age had reduced him to a fraction of himself. A ghost, not a man.

C.J. forced his feet to move across the room, but the space seemed ten miles wide, every step taking ten minutes. One machine measured his father's blood pressure, heart rate, oxygen level. Another dispensed medicine, a third waited to release morphine. Above him, IV poles dripped steady droplets of saline and other things C.J. didn't recognize into John's veins. "Dad?" he said again.

His father turned toward him, moving a frame at a time, like a movie in slow motion. It took a moment for recognition to set in, and then his father's eyes widened. "Christopher?"

"Yes, it's me." C.J. pulled up a nearby chair and took a seat. He hesitated, afraid to disturb the fragile balance of medicine, machine and man. But then his father's hand slid across the sea of white and reached for C.J.'s. Paper-thin skin, cold, but still it held the root of firmness, of the man he used to be.

"I'm glad you came, son." His father paused, drew in a breath that ended on a shudder. "Surprised you came."

"Me, too," C.J. admitted. He hadn't, in fact, even been sure he was going to go through with seeing his father until he'd actually rung the doorbell. "I wanted you to meet my daughter."

"I'm a...grandfather?"

The light in John's eyes told C.J. he had been right to come and to bring Sarah. She should know her grandfather, after all, even if it was at the end of his life. C.J. didn't know how much time his father had, but found himself already hoping for more.

"Her name is Sarah. She's six. And absolutely perfect, of course." C.J. chuckled.

"Tell me about her," his father said.

In John's eyes, C.J. read genuine interest. Maybe it was seeing the end of his life approaching so close, maybe it was regrets catching up with him. Maybe it was simply that he had a grandchild, but something had turned John from a distant bystander in C.J.'s life to a vested player. And so he did as his father asked, telling John everything—about attempting Sarah's ponytails, and buying the Doctor Barbie for Cassidy, and setting up the Winterfest, and playing Santa.

"*You* did all that?"

"Yeah. I kind of got talked into the Santa part. But it was fun and I was glad I did it. It sort of made up for—" C.J. cut off the sentence.

Silence cut between them. His father's hand slackened on C.J.'s, then he bit his lip, let out a breath and refocused his grip. "For all those Christmases you never had."

Beside him, the morphine timer clicked on and began to dispense its automatic dose of pain medication.

C.J. cleared his throat. "That's all in the past, Dad."

With his free hand, his father folded the blanket over his stomach, then folded it again before meeting his son's eyes. "I'm sorry, Christopher. I was a lousy father. I don't even know if there's enough adjectives for how terrible I was, how self-centered I was in those years."

C.J. didn't say anything. He could have taken the opportunity to scream and yell, let loose with thirty-plus years of blame, but what would be the point now? There was no going back and undoing what had been done. And so he waited, hoping that his father's apology would be followed by the answer to why.

His father worked at the blanket for a moment more, then pushed the edge away and heaved a sigh. "When I lost your mother, I couldn't handle being a parent. It was like I lost my compass when she died and I didn't know what to do with you, so I did…nothing." John's features crumbled, and for the first time ever, C.J. saw true regret take over his father's face. "I can't change any of that now, as much as I wish I could, but I can tell you to be better than I was. Bad advice, but it's all I've got. I'm sorry, C.J." His father's grip trembled. "I'm sorry."

"It's all right, Dad. It's all right." He squeezed his father's hand, and realized that it was. He'd turned out okay, hadn't he? Not a criminal, not a drug addict, but a responsible, tax-paying citizen with a career and a future. And now, a child.

What good was bitterness going to do him? What good had it done any of them? "I forgive you."

When the morphine had gone into John's system, C.J. had seen the tightening in his father's shoulders and jaw lessen, as the medication relieved some of his pain. But what the pharmaceutical industry had done was nothing compared to the effect those three words had. Everything about his father's body seemed to relax, as if a ten-thousand-pound weight had been lifted from his back, and the hardness that C.J. had always associated with John was whisked away in an instant.

John's watery eyes met his son's, filled with disbelief at first, then gratitude. "Thank you, Christopher," his father said, his voice breaking, "thank you."

All C.J. could do was nod, and battle against the lump that had lodged in his throat.

After a long moment John sighed. "I guess I was never really ready to be a father."

Hadn't C.J. said the same thing, or at least thought it, a dozen times over the past week? "Maybe you're never ready for a thing like that. All you can do is the best you're able."

A knock sounded on the door, then Paula entered the room with Sarah by her side. "Someone wants to meet you."

A tiny bit of peanut butter lingered on the corner of Sarah's lips, which made C.J. and John chuckle. C.J. scooped up his daughter, whisked off the peanut butter, then brought her over to his father's side. "This is your grandfather, John," he said.

"Are you sick?" Sarah asked. Always direct, clearly a little of Kiki and a lot of C.J. in her.

John nodded, but smiled, too. "But it's not something you can catch."

That seemed to satisfy Sarah. She sat down on C.J.'s lap in the chair, and after a few minutes, started chattering about her life in Riverbend, as comfortable with John as she would be with anyone. The longer his daughter talked, the more amazed C.J. became at the transformation he saw in his father. The distance between the two men seemed to close even more as Sarah talked, telling her stories and including them both in her conversations about Christmas and unicorns, making them laugh, as if her words were the balm they'd each needed.

Jessica had been right. Sarah was the perfect medicine for what had been ailing this broken relationship.

CHAPTER ELEVEN

RIVERBEND was silent. Jessica parked her car downtown, in the same spot as the night before, only now the town was quiet, everyone buttoned down for Christmas Eve, families gathered together, counting their blessings.

A bone-deep ache pierced Jessica and she sucked in a breath, but it did nothing to assuage the pain. She wanted some of what so many of those in Riverbend had. A family. A child.

A life to come home to.

She'd had that with Dennis, but always it had been missing that one more element.

By choice, she knew. But now, if she could go back and do it over again—

But the past was where it was, and all she had was what lay ahead.

Jessica began to stroll through the silent town park toward Santa's Village, drawing her coat tight against the cold. The lights C.J. had set up still twinkled, but the people were gone, the carolers all at home, the band members probably wearing their flannel pajamas, their bellies full of hot chocolate.

The animals had been returned to whatever zoo or farm normally housed them, all except for Dash, who was happily antler-deep in his feed bin, munching a mix of hay and grain. Jessica called Dash over to the edge of the pen, then fished out a carrot stick and fed it to the skittish animal, who snagged it out of her hand, then hurried to the other side of the pen to munch in privacy.

"I don't blame you," she said to the reindeer. "That's pretty much how I like to operate. Stick to your own self and that way no one ever gets hurt."

She draped her arms over the wooden fence post and sighed. "But that hasn't worked out so well for me, huh?" She picked a splinter out of the wood and tossed it to the ground. "What's that old saying about jumping off a bridge? Either you do it with both feet or you wind up watching all the other boats pass you by?"

Jessica pushed off from the fence. "Well, I'm done standing on the bridge. I'm ready to leap."

Dash didn't provide so much as a hoof stomp in response. He stared at her. Probably thought she needed therapy for standing in the cold, talking to a reindeer in the middle of the night.

She glanced at her watch. It was nearly midnight. Far too late to show up on C.J.'s doorstep and tell him that a meaningful conversation with a reindeer had changed her mind about taking risks and standing still. Tomorrow, she decided, would be soon enough.

"Mrs. Patterson, aren't you supposed to be on a beach somewhere?"

Jessica turned at the sound of Earl Klein's voice. "Oh, yeah. I, ah, missed the snow."

He chuckled. "I knew you couldn't take the Christmas out of the Claus. Glad you came back."

She smiled. "I am, too. What are you doing out here at this time of night?"

"Checking on the reindeer. C.J. asked me to keep an eye on him until the reindeer farm picks him up on the twenty-sixth. They had a little incident with the other reindeer. Apparently a few of 'em tried to make a break for it." Earl leaned in, cupped a hand over his mouth, as if Dash might overhear their conversation. "I suspect they were trying to get to the North Pole in time for Christmas. Anyway, they busted down a fence, got all riled up, and the place asked if we could keep Dash till they had a chance to get it fixed. Then I s'ppose I'll have to run the reindeer on up with my truck and trailer."

"C.J. isn't going to do it?"

"He can't. He's not here anymore."

"Not here…?" Cold ice sank to the pit of Jessica's stomach, a hard block that cut off her air, her thoughts. "He's gone?"

Already?

"Yep. Pulled out of here early this morning. Didn't say where he was going. 'Course, I ain't his momma, so I wouldn't expect him to keep his calendar with me or anything like that."

"Of course." Jessica rubbed her hands together, suddenly chilled to the bone. She was too late. She'd missed her opportunity with C.J., with Sarah. "I should get home." But home no longer held the appeal it had just a few minutes earlier. She should have stayed in Miami. Stayed on the plane. Stayed in her car.

Done anything not to have heard Earl say that C.J. had already left.

"That's a good idea," Earl said. "Everyone should be home on Christmas Eve. Even old men like me." He reached into a bin, pulled out some feed for Dash, making sure the reindeer had plenty of food and water to get him through the night, then tipped his cap Jessica's way. "Good night, Mrs. Claus. Merry Christmas."

"Merry Christmas, Earl." But for the first time, when Jessica said the words, they had lost their holiday ring.

* * *

C.J. had been walking for half an hour, wandering the streets of Riverbend, thinking. After a while he found himself exactly where he expected to end up—in the middle of his own creation.

The Winterfest.

The park was silent. Everyone in town was at home, the carousel still, the vendors gone, the food carts empty. The entire park had an eerie, almost tomblike feeling to it.

Yet it was as familiar to C.J. as the back of his own hand. He knew this empty shell. It was a set, the back of the Hollywood image, after the actors had gone home, the cameras were turned off, and the charade had been exposed as nothing more than smoke and mirrors.

Everything here had been part of creating that Christmas dream—everything a facade, except for one very real, breathing element—

C.J. stopped and sucked in a deep gulp of cold air. *Jessica.*

He crossed the snow-covered lawn in several quick strides, reaching out and grasping her shoulder to stop her before she could disappear and turn into a figment of his imagination. "Jessica?"

She turned and when she did, the moonlight caught her face, reflecting little glints of silver on her cheeks. "C.J.?"

"Why are you crying?"

"I…I thought you were gone."

"I was, but I came back. And…so did you, I see." She was here, and he'd been so sure she'd stay in Florida and skip Christmas entirely. "Did you get sunburned?"

It was a stupid question, but he asked it because he was afraid to ask the real ones. Had she come back because she wanted him—or because she wanted to say goodbye?

She shrugged, but then her tears gave way to a smile. "I missed the snow. I missed the town." A pause. A heartbeat. "I missed you."

Now his heart soared, and C.J. realized no one in Hollywood would ever be able to write a line of dialogue that could be as perfect as those three words. "I missed you, too." Then he caught her hands with his. "Where are your gloves? You never have any gloves on."

"I came straight from the airport. I didn't need gloves in Miami, silly."

"Good. Because that means I can warm you up." He pressed her cold fingertips to his lips and blew lightly on them. "Better?"

"Much." Then she looked around. "Where's Sarah?"

"LuAnn came over after I got back to the apartment tonight. She said she likes Kiki's TV better than hers, but I think she was looking for an excuse to kick me out of the house so I could…" He grinned. "Well, I guess so I could go looking for you. All the way to Miami if necessary."

"A little matchmaking at work?"

"She told me she thought we made a pretty good married couple."

"Married couple?"

"Mr. and Mrs. Claus."

"Oh, yeah. That."

For a second C.J. wondered if he'd made a mistake. After all, Jessica's original Santa had died. Was it rude to even suggest he could replace him? "I'm sorry, Jessica, I didn't mean—"

"No, don't." She pressed her fingers to his lips. "You're fine. I thought we were good together, too. Maybe we should take the show on the road."

He chuckled. "Sonny and Cher, only in Santa suits?"

"The only problem with that is I can't sing."

"That would present a dilemma." He rubbed his thumbs over her hands, then looked up to meet her eyes. He needed to tell her a thousand different things. He'd start at the beginning and hope she wanted to stay with him, right to the end. "You were right. I went and saw my father, yesterday—that's where I've been—and brought Sarah to meet him. We may not have fixed everything, but we came close enough."

She smiled. "I'm happy for you, C.J. I really am."

"I have more to tell you, Jessica, so much more. About Sarah, and our relationship and—"

Her hand went to his mouth, stopping his words. "I have something to say first. I made a decision tonight. I'm going to sell the store to Mindy."

"Sell Santa's Workshop? You can't do that."

"Mindy loves it, too, and I'm sure she'll do a wonderful job running it. Plus, I have plenty of great employees who'll help her."

"But…but why would you do that?"

"I got down to Miami, slapped on my sunscreen, ordered my mai tai and realized I didn't want any of it, heck, didn't want anything here or there, not without you. None of this—" Jessica swept an arm in a semicircle, indicating the town "—matters at all if I don't have you in my life. You and Sarah. I'm tired of being afraid of what might happen, C.J., because I already realized the worst that could happen."

"What's that?"

A wobbly smile took over her face. "I could lose you. And I don't care if we have ten years together or twenty or a hundred. I'm not going to live life any longer waiting for the other shoe to drop. I've already been through the worst, and I survived."

Winter swirled a dusting of flakes around them, a gust of light wind. A Christmas-light rainbow twinkled in Jessica's hair, danced across her features, giving her an ethereal, magical edge. C.J. traced along the edge of her jaw, loving her more in that moment than he'd ever thought he could. "But you're Mrs. Claus. And I live in California."

"I bet they need Mrs. Clauses out there, too. And if moving out west is what it takes to leap off the bridge and finally have the life I really want, then that's where I'll go. Because it's where you are."

She'd given it all up, for him. The store. The town. Even the snow.

C.J. roared with laughter. "I can't believe you did that."

"I just threw away my business and you're *laughing?*" There was no merriment in her face now, only frustration.

"Oh, Jessica, not over that, but because—" he waited a second to catch his breath, the humor and the irony too much "—because on the way back from my father's house, I quit my job. Told them I was moving to Riverbend, Indiana, to take up permanent residence in Santa's Village."

It took about five seconds for the irony to hit her, too, and then Jessica started to laugh. "Oh, no, you didn't."

"I did. The director asked me if I wanted the name of his shrink. And if that one didn't work out, he offered the name of his Chihuahua's shrink, too."

"Why would you do that?"

He drew in a breath, feeling the frosty air ice every inch of his windpipe, all the way to his lungs. And loving the feeling, the very real, very tangible feeling of cold. "Let me show you something." He took her hand and led her across the lawn, beside the gazebo and over to the gingerbread family.

A mother, a father and two gingerbread children, all made out of a flexible polymer that allowed them to move. Lights blinked under their gumdrop buttons, in their candy eyes. Their arms waved up and down, their bodies twisted side to side and their smiles were wide and happy. The two gingerbread children held hands and waved their clasped arms back and forth with a whispered mechanical whine.

"I think this is my favorite display. It's so cool how you made them move and yet look so lifelike." Jessica grinned. "Especially considering they're, well, cookies."

He chuckled. "Let me show you something." He led her around to the back of the display to expose the family's secrets. Wires, computer chips, animatronics, tucked into hollow bellies and mindless dummies. "It's all fake. None of it's real. I build these things. Create imaginary worlds. And yes, they're amazing, but they're nowhere as amazing as the world I found here. In Riverbend." He looked around the park, as far as he could see. "*This* is real. *You* are real and genuine. What I had in California, that world, is as fake as these gingerbread people, and when I met you, for the first time I found something that made me get honest with myself. Scared the pants off me, but eventually I came around."

"And because of that, you want to stay here, with the snow and the cold?"

"I'd stay in Alaska or Mexico or anywhere, as long as you were there, for one simple reason." He captured her face in his palms and met her emerald gaze with his own. "I love you, Jessica. And it may sound crazy, but I fell in love with you over the mayonnaise."

"And here I thought it was my wheat bread," she said, then snuggled into his embrace. She fit perfectly, and he held her tight, dreaming of a future he'd never thought a man like him could have. "I love you, too, C.J."

His world had come full circle. A week ago C.J. had been a man adrift, alone. Now he was a father, and a man with a future. A home. He could dream of a front porch, a dinner waiting for him on the table, someone greeting him—no, now two someones—at the end of the day. His eyes stung, and he held Jessica even tighter, wondering if even she knew how incredibly blessed he felt right now.

The town hall clock struck midnight, one gong after another announcing the arrival of Christmas Day. "We better get home," he said. "Because it's

Christmas, and I believe there's one more tree left to decorate."

"On one condition," she said, taking his hand and joining him as they left the park. "That you and Sarah spend Christmas at my house. I believe we still need to give her an incredible Christmas."

"Done. I still haven't mastered the cooking thing yet, and I could use a little help in the kitchen."

She laughed. "Well, we have a problem there. Because my choices are still tuna or—"

"Tuna," he finished, joining her laughter. "I'll bring some stuff from my cupboards, which are admittedly pretty lean, too, but at least I have ham and cheese." As they reached the edge of the park, he turned back and gave the Winterfest one more look. It was missing…something. "Next year, how about if we add fireworks?"

"It's always going to be about going bigger and better with you, C. J. Hamilton, isn't it?"

C.J. returned his gaze to the woman he loved and realized in one area of his life, he already had perfection. "Only when it comes to Christmas."

Then he kissed Mrs. Claus, with a whisper about the plans Santa had for the year to come, plans that were just for the two of them. From somewhere at the back of the park, Dash stomped his hoof in indignation about not being included.

EPILOGUE

"A UNICORN with a Santa hat!" Sarah clutched the stuffed toy to her chest and beamed. "It's perfect, Daddy and Jessica! I love it!"

C.J. laughed, accepted his hundredth hug of the morning, then watched as his daughter ran and gave Jessica the same. He could get used to this, very easily.

After leaving the town park, C.J. and Jessica had stopped by her store to load up on even more toys and gifts for Sarah, knowing they were spoiling the girl, but laughing and enjoying it, anyway. Then C.J. had managed to carry a sleeping Sarah over to Jessica's house and sneak her into the guest bedroom. When she'd awoken Christmas morning, he'd told her Santa had whisked her off to Jessica's, which had duly impressed the six-year-old.

Now Jessica's living room was littered with wrapping paper. Sarah was surrounded by a sea of presents, most of them from C.J. and Jessica, a few of the bigger ones from Santa himself. The little girl hurried from one toy to the other, playing with each for a few seconds before moving on to the next, exclaiming over and over again that this one was her new favorite.

"I think we might have gone overboard," Jessica said, joining C.J. where he stood by the Christmas tree and handing him a much-needed cup of coffee. He loved the way she looked in her candy-cane-printed flannel pajamas, and knew someday soon, he'd find out how she looked *under* them.

"Maybe we should scale it back next year." He grinned, watching Sarah's delight. "Maybe."

"I'm glad I decided to keep the shop after all. I think I'm going to need to increase my inventory just to keep up with your ideas, Mr. Hamilton."

He chuckled. "Don't worry. Once I get my construction business running out here, I'll be able to fund my own toy workshop. And I'll build 'em—"

"Bigger and better." They both laughed.

"Speaking of bigger and better," C.J. said. "Or rather, just right." He reached into the tree and pulled out the present he'd hidden there last night. He'd had it ever since he'd left Ohio, when he'd made up his mind that he wouldn't lose Jessica, even if he had to track her down in Florida.

Earlier this morning, he'd given Jessica a pair of

gloves, but that hadn't been the real gift. This one he'd held back, not sure of her answer, but knowing that he couldn't wait another second to ask.

Jessica turned and when she did, she saw the small velvet box and gasped. "C.J.—"

"I know we've only known each other for a few days. But I've waited all my life to find someone to love, someone who would love me, too. And I don't want to wait anymore." He pulled back the lid, revealing a trio of round diamonds, nestled close together. "I bought this because it's like holly berries—"

"And old legends say that the holly was the masculine plant, using its thorns to protect the lady." She smiled in wonderment, then reached out a finger and traced the design he'd carved into the band. "The ivy symbolized the woman because it embraced everything it touched."

"That's what you did for me, Jessica. You embraced me and you made me feel like I'd come home." He took the ring out of the box, held it over her left hand, hoping that he hadn't gone too far, moved too fast, done something insane. "Will you marry me?"

Beside them, Sarah went on playing, completely unaware of the life-changing events happening on the other side of the sofa. C.J.'s heart stopped beating, his breath lodged in his throat.

Jessica's emerald gaze met his, and before she

even opened her mouth, he knew her answer. "Yes, C.J. I'll marry you."

He slid the ring onto her finger, the holly and the ivy entwining along the gold band, then leaned forward and kissed her. A sweet kiss, nothing like what he really wanted to give her, because Sarah was a few feet away. Later, there would be time. Plenty of time.

"I have a present for you, too," she said, blushing a little. "You didn't exactly give me a lot of time to shop, so it's not much, but—" Jessica bent down, then withdrew a gift from beneath the tree and handed it to C.J.

"Hmmm…socks? A tie?"

"Stop kidding and just open it." Her ring sparkled in the overhead light, but her smile held a higher wattage.

C.J. grinned, then did as she said and unwrapped the long, skinny box and pulled off the cover. Inside was a Christmas stocking made of red velvet, topped with white, with his name written across the top in twisted gold rope. "A stocking?"

Jessica reached out a hand, then drew C.J. over to the fireplace. Together they hung the stocking on a hook jutting from the mantel, nestling it between Jessica's and Sarah's. He was part of the family now, a permanent part.

Then she turned to him, and in her smile C.J. saw the home he'd sought all his life. "This way," Jessica said, "Santa will always find you."

* * * * *

SPECIAL EDITION

Life, Love and Family

*These contemporary romances will strike a chord
with you as heroines juggle life
and relationships on their way to true love.*

New York Times *bestselling author*
Linda Lael Miller
*brings you a BRAND-NEW contemporary story
featuring her fan-favorite McKettrick family.*

Meg McKettrick is surprised to be reunited
with her high school flame, Brad O'Ballivan.
After enjoying a career as a country-and-
western singer, Brad aches for a home and
family…and seeing Meg again makes him
realize he still loves her. But their pride
manages to interfere with love…until an unexpected matchmaker gets involved.

*Turn the page for a sneak preview of
THE McKETTRICK WAY by Linda Lael Miller
On sale November 20, wherever books are sold.*

Brad shoved the truck into gear and drove to the bottom of the hill, where the road forked. Turn left, and he'd be home in five minutes. Turn right, and he was headed for Indian Rock.

He had no damn business going to Indian Rock.

He had nothing to say to Meg McKettrick, and if he never set eyes on the woman again, it would be two weeks too soon.

He turned right.

He couldn't have said why.

He just drove straight to the Dixie Dog Drive-In.

Back in the day, he and Meg used to meet at the Dixie Dog, by tacit agreement, when either of them had been away. It had been some kind of universe thing, purely intuitive.

Passing familiar landmarks, Brad told himself he ought to turn around. The old days were gone. Things had ended badly between him and Meg anyhow, and she wasn't going to be at the Dixie Dog.

He kept driving.

He rounded a bend, and there was the Dixie Dog. Its big neon sign, a giant hot dog, was all lit up and going through its corny sequence—first it was covered in red squiggles of light, meant to suggest ketchup, and then yellow, for mustard.

Brad pulled into one of the slots next to a speaker, rolled down the truck window and ordered.

A girl roller-skated out with the order about five minutes later.

When she wheeled up to the driver's window, smiling, her eyes went wide with recognition, and she dropped the tray with a clatter.

Silently Brad swore. Damn if he hadn't forgotten he was a famous country singer.

The girl, a skinny thing wearing too much eye makeup, immediately started to cry. "I'm sorry!" she sobbed, squatting to gather up the mess.

"It's okay," Brad answered quietly, leaning to look down at her, catching a glimpse of her plastic name tag. "It's okay, Mandy. No harm done."

"I'll get you another dog and a shake right away, Mr. O'Ballivan!"

"Mandy?"

She stared up at him pitifully, sniffling. Thanks

to the copious tears, most of the goop on her eyes had slid south. "Yes?"

"When you go back inside, could you not mention seeing me?"

"But you're Brad O'Ballivan!"

"Yeah," he answered, suppressing a sigh. "I know."

She rolled a little closer. "You wouldn't happen to have a picture you could autograph for me, would you?"

"Not with me," Brad answered.

"You could sign this napkin, though," Mandy said. "It's only got a little chocolate on the corner."

Brad took the paper napkin and her order pen, and scrawled his name. Handed both items back through the window.

She turned and whizzed back toward the side entrance to the Dixie Dog.

Brad waited, marveling that he hadn't considered incidents like this one before he'd decided to come back home. In retrospect, it seemed shortsighted, to say the least, but the truth was, he'd expected to be—Brad O'Ballivan.

Presently Mandy skated back out again, and this time she managed to hold on to the tray.

"I didn't tell a soul!" she whispered. "But Heather and Darlene *both* asked me why my mascara was all smeared." Efficiently she hooked the tray onto the bottom edge of the window.

Brad extended payment, but Mandy shook her head.

"The boss said it's on the house, since I dumped your first order on the ground."

He smiled. "Okay, then. Thanks."

Mandy retreated, and Brad was just reaching for the food when a bright red Blazer whipped into the space beside his. The driver's door sprang open, crashing into the metal speaker, and somebody got out in a hurry.

Something quickened inside Brad.

And in the next moment Meg McKettrick was standing practically on his running board, her blue eyes blazing.

Brad grinned. "I guess you're not over me after all," he said.

▼ Silhouette®

SPECIAL EDITION™

brings you a heartwarming
new McKettrick's story from

NEW YORK TIMES BESTSELLING AUTHOR

LINDA LAEL
MILLER

THE
McKETTRICK
Way

Meg McKettrick is surprised to be reunited
with her high school flame, Brad O'Ballivan,
who has returned home to his family's
neighboring ranch. After seeing Meg again,
Brad realizes he still loves her. But the pride
of both manage to interfere with love...until
an unexpected matchmaker gets involved.

—— McKettrick Women ——

Available December wherever you buy books.

SPECIAL EDITION™

Life, Love and Family

**These contemporary romances
will strike a chord with you
as heroines juggle
life and relationships
on their way to true love.**

Enjoy 6 new titles each month,
from Silhouette Special Edition,
available wherever books are sold,
including most bookstores,
supermarkets, discount stores
and drugstores.

REQUEST YOUR FREE BOOKS!

2 FREE NOVELS PLUS 2
FREE GIFTS!

HARLEQUIN ROMANCE®

From the Heart, For the Heart

YES! Please send me 2 FREE Harlequin Romance® novels and my 2 FREE gifts. After receiving them, if I don't wish to receive any more books, I can return the shipping statement marked "cancel." If I don't cancel, I will receive 4 brand-new novels every month and be billed just $3.57 per book in the U.S., or $4.05 per book in Canada, plus 25¢ shipping and handling per book and applicable taxes, if any*. That's a savings of over 15% off the cover price! I understand that accepting the 2 free books and gifts places me under no obligation to buy anything. I can always return a shipment and cancel at any time. Even if I never buy another book from Harlequin, the two free books and gifts are mine to keep forever.   114 HDN EEV7 314 HDN EEWK

Name	(PLEASE PRINT)	
Address		Apt.
City	State/Prov.	Zip/Postal Code

Signature (if under 18, a parent or guardian must sign)

Mail to the **Harlequin Reader Service®**:
IN U.S.A.: P.O. Box 1867, Buffalo, NY 14240-1867
IN CANADA: P.O. Box 609, Fort Erie, Ontario L2A 5X3

Not valid to current Harlequin Romance subscribers.

Want to try two free books from another line?
Call 1-800-873-8635 or visit www.morefreebooks.com.

* Terms and prices subject to change without notice. NY residents add applicable sales tax. Canadian residents will be charged applicable provincial taxes and GST. This offer is limited to one order per household. All orders subject to approval. Credit or debit balances in a customer's account(s) may be offset by any other outstanding balance owed by or to the customer. Please allow 4 to 6 weeks for delivery.

Your Privacy: Harlequin is committed to protecting your privacy. Our Privacy Policy is available online at www.eHarlequin.com or upon request from the Reader Service. From time to time we make our lists of customers available to reputable firms who may have a product or service of interest to you. If you would prefer we not share your name and address, please check here. ☐

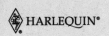

Every great love has a story to tell™

Martin Collins was the man
Keti Whitechapen had always loved but
just couldn't marry. But one Christmas Eve
Keti finds a dog she names Marley.
That night she has a dream about
Christmas past. And Christmas present—
and future. A future that could include the
man she's continued to love.

Look for

A Spirit of Christmas

by

Margot Early

Available December wherever you buy books.

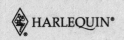

HARLEQUIN®

American ★ Romance®

Kate Merrill had grown up convinced
that the most attractive men were incapable
of ever settling down. Yet the harder she
resisted the superstar photographer
Tyler Nichols, the more persistent the
handsome world traveler became.
So by the time Christmas arrived, there
was only one wish on her holiday list—
that she was wrong!

LOOK FOR

THE CHRISTMAS DATE

BY

Michele Dunaway

**Available December
wherever you buy books**

Coming Next Month

In a month filled with Christmas sparkle, we bring you tycoons
and bosses, loves lost and found, little miracles that change your life
and always, always a happy ending!

#3991 SNOWBOUND WITH MR. RIGHT Judy Christenberry
Mistletoe & Marriage

Sally loves Christmastime in the small town of Bailey, with the snow
softly falling and all the twinkling lights on the trees. But when handsome
stranger and city slicker Hunter arrives, everything seems different, and
she is in danger of losing her heart.

#3992 THE MILLIONAIRE TYCOON'S ENGLISH ROSE Lucy Gordon
The Rinucci Brothers

Ever heard the expression, to love someone is to set them free? Freedom
is precious to Celia, since she can't see. But she can live life to the full!
The last of the Rinucci brothers, Francesco, wants to wrap her in cotton
wool, but hadn't bargained on feisty Celia....

#3993 THE BOSS'S LITTLE MIRACLE Barbara McMahon

Career girl Anna doesn't have time for love. She's poised for promotion,
when in walks her new CEO, Tanner...the man who broke her heart a few
weeks ago! Then Anna discovers a little miracle has happened—and it
changes everything.

#3994 THEIR GREEK ISLAND REUNION Carol Grace

Even the most perfect relationships have cracks—as Olivia and Jack have
realized. Their marriage seems over, but Jack refuses to let go. He whisks
Olivia away to an idyllic Greek island. But will it be enough to give them a
forever-future together?

#3995 WIN, LOSE...OR WED! Melissa McClone

Love it or loathe it, reality TV is here to stay! Millie loathes it, after
irresistible bachelor Jace dumped her in front of millions of viewers. But in
aid of charity, she finds herself on a new show with Jace, and *everything* is
captured on camera—even their stolen kisses!

#3996 HIS CHRISTMAS ANGEL Michelle Douglas

Do you remember *that* guy? The one from your past that you loved
more than life itself, the one you never seem to be able to get over?
Imagine he's back in town, and more gorgeous than ever. Join Cassie
as boy-next-door Sol comes home for Christmas....

HRCNM1107